Eleven Year Reunion

Three Rivers Ranch Romance™
Book 10

Liz Isaacson

"I will say of the Lord, He is my refuge and my fortress: my God; in him will I trust."

PSALMS 91:2

Chapter One

The sun had never looked so bright to Grace Lewis. Of course, she rarely saw the sun rise, what with arriving at work by three a.m. for the past several years. *The life of a pastry chef*, she thought as she turned out of her driveway and headed north.

She drove slowly, not wanting to arrive out at Three Rivers before everyone else. But she already knew she would. She'd been up since three a.m.—old habits and all that. She'd baked a loaf of bread that now rode shotgun next to her and would become lunch once noon rolled around.

By then, Grace would be ready for her afternoon siesta, but she didn't expect to be done in the kitchen that early. Heidi Ackerman had promised it would be a long day of baking, tasting, tweaking, and testing.

Grace couldn't be more excited.

She eased up on the gas pedal when she realized her enthusiasm over today's adventures had caused her to speed up. She enjoyed the leisurely drive through the crisp fall air, her thoughts wandering.

And when they did that, they almost always journeyed down south to Dallas. A frown tugged at Grace's mouth, and she did her best to straighten her lips again. So she failed in Dallas. Big deal. Many cupcakeries failed on their first try. At least that was what her instructors had warned the group of pastry chefs that had graduated from the Pastry and Baking School at New York's Institute of Culinary Education.

Still, Grace had thought sure she'd outbake the odds. She'd moved back to Dallas, gotten up at two a.m. for weeks perfecting her cupcake recipes. She painted the shop. Ordered the tables and display cases. Saw to every detail.

She'd made it eight months before admitting she couldn't put another month's rent on her credit card.

"Don't focus on that," she coached herself as she continued down the two-lane highway. She didn't want her thoughts to spiral right before she had to rely on her sharp wit and impeccable palate. If she allowed herself to continue down that particular train of thought, she'd end up obsessing over how she should've chosen a better location or entered more contests or started out of her kitchen before trying for retail space.

As the miles and minutes passed, she refocused her thoughts on the blessings that had led her to Three Rivers. Her friendship with Chelsea Ackerman—now Chelsea Marshall with two kids and a quiet life on a ranch she'd never wanted—made Grace smile.

It also reminded her of the boy she'd left behind in Oklahoma City. She banished those thoughts before they could even take root, beyond relieved when she saw the sign indicating a left turn for Three Rivers Ranch up ahead.

She maneuvered onto the dirt road, wishing she'd considered what the drive out to the ranch would do to her little car before she'd taken the job with Heidi. But it didn't matter. She wasn't in Dallas anymore and she still had the opportunity to work with baked goods. She'd be Heidi's head pastry chef any day, under any road conditions.

Grace pulled around the corner and the homestead Chelsea had described spread before her. Two homes, sprawling yards, a facility with a beautiful sign that read "Courage Reins," and new construction going in on the west side of the road. She passed that first, noticing that the construction workers were already out and busy.

Of course they would be, she thought. They didn't want to work in the Texas heat any longer than necessary, though it was October and starting to cool off.

She parked where Heidi had instructed, noting that she was indeed the first to arrive. Not wanting to wait in the car, she got out and took a deep breath of clean, ranch air. Chelsea had told her there was nothing like it—and Grace had to agree.

With a smile flirting with her lips, she headed for the homestead that would be Heidi's test kitchen for the next several weeks. Her son, Squire, now lived in the homestead, but his wife, Kelly, had insisted that Heidi come out and use the large kitchen to test her recipes. After all, Heidi's condo in town wasn't fit for four women to be baking in at the same time.

With no one but the cowhands and the construction crew stirring, Grace skirted the perimeter of the yard, thinking she'd take a short walk out to the fields and back. Someone surely would show up by the time she returned.

She noticed the calving stalls and chicken coops to her right. Beyond them lay the silos and a couple of barns and way down on the end, a large, portable building. Behind all of that sat a row of cabins, presumably for the cowboys who worked the ranch.

To her left sat the homestead, with its sweeping lawn and full vegetable garden, along with an obviously new swing set and shed. The tamed land eventually gave way to the wild range, and Grace paused on the edge of the two pieces. She felt the same as the waving prairie grasses—without shape or form or worry or care. At the same time, she longed to be molded and cultured into something beautiful. Longed to be needed. Longed to be successful.

She turned back to the homestead, wishing she knew how to become the person she wanted to be. She'd prayed for help, for guidance, for answers.

And God had sent her to Three Rivers to test recipes with a retired woman who wanted to open a bakery in town. A woman who had explained to Grace that she'd given up her dream of owning a bakery almost thirty-five years ago.

Grace took another deep breath as she heard Heidi tell her that she hadn't really given up the bakery. God had promised her she'd have it one day. She'd decided to trust in Him, and Grace admired the older woman's patience and faith.

She stuffed her hands in her pockets as she headed for the house. Heidi had told her to take the steps up to the deck and enter through the French doors. As she aimed herself in that direction, something glinted out of the corner of her eye.

Around the steps, under the deck, waited a patio. And on that patio, a guitar rested in a rocking chair.

Her fingers suddenly itched to play. She hadn't taken her guitar to New York with her, and she'd abandoned the instrument completely as she struggled to launch her cupcakery. But now....

Her feet seemed to change direction without instruction from her brain. She picked up the guitar, a small thread of guilt pulling through her, and sat on the edge of the rocker. Her fingers found the strings easily, pressed chords from muscle memory, and she began to play.

She'd hummed her way through her favorite tune, and was gearing up to sing the lyrics when someone said, "What do you think you're doing?"

Grace almost dropped the guitar. She fumbled it, her hands finally finding purchase on the neck and saving it from clattering to the cement.

Good thing, too, because she didn't think the glowering cowboy standing on the steps she'd come down would've appreciated her dropping his guitar. He definitely didn't need to vocalize that he owned it. His offensive stance and folded arms said that.

"I'm—I'm sorry." Grace stood and replaced the guitar in the rocking chair. The man continued to glower, his square jaw boxy and tight. "I was waiting for Heidi to show up, and I just saw your guitar, and—it's a real fine instrument. You must take good care of it."

Of course, leaving it outside in a chair didn't testify of such things, but Grace swallowed those words. She wished she had her own cowboy hat to cover her hair and eyes, or that he would move so she could scamper past him and get upstairs and into her safe place: the kitchen.

"What song was that?" He didn't sound like he was about to snap, and the muscles in Grace's neck relaxed.

"Just something my daddy used to sing."

"I've heard it before."

Grace really didn't think so, but she didn't want to argue with the cowboy. He seemed so tall and imposing, standing on the third step as he did. And she was a tall woman at nearly five-feet-ten-inches.

His arms relaxed; his hands fell to his sides.

"You work here?" she asked.

"Workin' on the new horse training facilities."

Ah, so he was a carpenter. Grace had a soft spot for woodworkers—the boy she'd known in Oklahoma City had been a builder. Or at least his daddy had been, and Jon was set to take over the business once his dad was ready to retire.

Grace once again wiped the memories from her mind. It wasn't uncommon for her to think of what might've been with Jonathan Carver. She'd been infatuated with him, overjoyed to go to the homecoming dance with him, and then devastated when her family moved to Dallas before she could really find out if she and Jon were a match.

She had only been seventeen at the time, but still. Something about him had stuck with Grace through all these years.

Moving forward to go past him, she said, "Well, I should—"

He stepped in front of her. "Grace Lewis?"

She peered up into his face, searching for his identity. His dark blue eyes and strong features could've belonged to anyone. He swept his hat off his head to reveal dark brown hair—with a sliver of white in the front.

Her heart tripped over itself, then catapulted into her throat. "Jon?"

JONATHAN CARVER STARED at Grace Lewis, the girl he'd just started to fall for as a senior in high school when her family had moved. A slow grin stretched across his face. "It is you! I knew I'd heard that song before."

Without thinking, without considering, he stepped down to the patio and engulfed her in a Texas-sized embrace. Though she was tall, he still had a few inches on her, and her head fit nicely against his chest, right below his neck.

Suddenly everything about Three Rivers didn't

seem so distasteful. He'd come here against his will, because he worked well with Brett Murphy and he needed the money. But he didn't like Texas and wasn't planning on staying once the job was done. Problem was, nothing in Oklahoma City called to him either.

He'd been drifting for a few years, and he knew it. Didn't know how to anchor himself though. Didn't know if he cared to.

Heat bolted through him as Grace laughed and brought her hands sliding up his back. "It's so good to see you."

He stepped away, very aware of how hard his nerve endings had started firing. It felt as though the temperature had shot through the roof in only a few seconds.

"What are you doing here?"

She pointed up, toward the deck. "I told you. I'm here to test recipes with Heidi."

"Right," he said, listening now. He hadn't before, because his fury at seeing a woman fondling his guitar had deafened him momentarily. "She's startin' up a bakery, right?"

"In the new year," Grace said, her slate blue eyes dancing with light. He wanted to reach out and tug on one of her sandy blonde curls, the way he had in history class all those years ago. He fisted his fingers instead.

"I'm her head pastry chef," Grace continued, a note of pride in her voice.

Jon grinned at her. "You go to school the way you wanted to?"

"In New York and everything."

"That's real great, Gracie."

She stiffened at the childhood endearment, and Jon's smile faltered. His confidence plummeted, and he suddenly wanted to collect his guitar and head inside for his cup of coffee. "Well, I should go."

"Oh." She shuffled sideways. "Okay."

He grabbed his guitar as he passed the rocking chair, all thoughts of bringing his coffee to the patio and playing while his morning off slid on by vanishing with the presence of Grace. He wasn't sure why he was running away, only that he didn't want to play catch-up right now.

He paused at the door leading to the basement, where he temporarily lived with Brett. He turned back to Grace. "It was real good to see you."

She smiled at him, driving his pulse to near erratic proportions. "You too, Jon."

He nodded and slipped inside, his thoughts volleying around his mind with the speed of a bullet. He couldn't make any of them settle long enough to do more than breathe and walk. The door snicked closed behind him, and he forced himself to move into the galley kitchen to the right.

Don't look back, don't look back, he told himself as he reached for the coffee pot and poured himself a cup with slightly shaking hands.

By the time he added sugar and brought the mug to his lips, he allowed himself to glance out the glass door.

Grace had gone.

Relief and regret flowed through his bloodstream simultaneously. *Really?* He aimed the question toward the heavens. He hadn't wanted to come to Three Rivers. Made that clear to everyone. His parents. Brett. God.

But, in the end, he'd come, because he'd felt like maybe in Three Rivers he could find the piece of his life that had been missing.

He just hadn't expected it to be Grace Lewis.

Is that why you led me here?

God stayed strangely silent this time, which only unsettled Jon further.

A couple of hours later, the scent of chocolate filled the basement. Probably the whole ranch. Jon had steadfastly refused to leave the couch, where a sports reel had been playing for hours. His coffee had long gone cold and his stomach roared with the want of baked goods.

He'd heard footsteps in the kitchen above him for hours, but now he heard them moving down the stairs. Sure enough, a knock sounded on the door next to the kitchen.

"Come in," he said, thinking of how he would've acted if the person on the other side of the door had been Kelly. In fact, she regularly brought dinner down to him and Brett and neither of them got off the couch for her.

Jon knew, though, as soon as the door opened, that the bearer of delicious food was not Kelly.

"Heidi wanted me to bring some samples around." Grace perched on the edge of the couch, a plate overflowing with three different types of brownies. His mouth watered, and not just from the sight of the chocolatey goodness.

But from the woman holding it. Her skin held the hint of the summer sun's kiss, and he wanted nothing more than to touch it. His gaze settled on her lips as he wondered if she'd taste as sweet as the concoctions she'd brought.

"Jon?"

He blinked and snapped himself out of his fantasies. "Which do you recommend?"

"You should try them all." Her eyes held that

mysterious sparkle, the one that had first captured his attention in high school. Memories flooded him now. Memories he'd only been containing behind a thin wisp of plastic wrap because Grace wasn't physically in the room with him.

"Which first?" he ground out through a tight throat.

"The German chocolate is my favorite." She extended the plate closer to him, and he selected a particularly gooey brownie.

As he bit into it, he definitely decided that life in Three Rivers had just improved drastically.

Chapter Two

Grace watched Jon eat her brownies, supreme satisfaction singing through her when he moaned. "Good grief, Gracie," he said. "These are fantastic. You made these?"

She didn't even mind that he'd used her childhood nickname. She wasn't sure why annoyance had slipped through her earlier, though as she mixed eggs and milk with flour and cocoa she'd figured it out.

"Gracie" was who she'd been in Oklahoma City. Once she moved to Dallas, she'd given up the nickname and hadn't looked back. But somehow, Jon calling her Gracie sang to her soul in a way nothing had since she'd arrived in New York and begun her dream of attending the Culinary Institute.

"It's my recipe, yes," Grace said. "Heidi added a secret ingredient to the mint one." She picked up one of the treats and passed it to him as he licked his fingers. Desire dove through her. She wanted his fingers in hers as they once had been, to pass through her hair as they once had, to stroke the side of her face right before he kissed her—as they once had.

She cleared her throat, relieved Jon seemed absorbed in devouring the brownies so he couldn't see the rising flush in her face.

"You okay?" he asked, and she flinched.

She nearly threw the plate of brownies at him and fled. "It's hot down here."

Jon watched her for a beat past comfortable, almost like he knew the temperature had nothing to do with the heat spiraling through her core. "What's that last one?"

"Double-chocolate fudge."

He groaned. "That might do me in." Still, he reached for the treat, and Grace noticed the size of his hands. Large, and calloused, and capable. When he drew back, she felt a sense of loss that made no sense.

She needed to go. Head out to the administration building—apparently the portable trailer on the end of the row she'd seen earlier—and pass out the rest of the treats to the cowhands. And come lunch, they'd all come up to the house to sample the cookies that Chelsea, Kelly, and Heidi were now mixing together.

Go, she told herself as Jon finished eating. *Go now*.

But she didn't move. Something magnetic emanated from Jon, pulled her in, kept her close.

"How long you in town?" he asked.

"I live here now," she said. "I moved here a few weeks ago to be Heidi's pastry chef."

A frown drew down his eyebrows and his focus slipped back to the TV. "Hm."

"You still in Oklahoma City?"

"Sometimes," he said, an answer that left her unsatisfied. He seemed closed off now that he'd eaten—completely the opposite of how most men reacted after they'd been fed something delicious.

Grace stood. "Well, come on up for lunch. We'll have sandwiches, salad, and more cookies than anyone can eat." She started for the glass door, almost desperate to escape when only moments ago she hadn't wanted to leave.

Her warring emotions almost drowned out Jon when he said, "What are you doin' for dinner?"

She spun, her heart back in her throat, her hope spiraling to ridiculous proportions. "Oh, I'm usually in bed by dinnertime." She gave a light laugh. "Getting up at three a.m. does that to a girl."

He stood now, his lean legs and strong arms more apparent when caged by low ceilings and close walls. "What time will you be done here, then?"

"I don't know. Sometime this afternoon, I suppose."

He moved closer, his blue eyes turning navy as he stalked closer. "I—Let's go grab something to eat whenever you're done. Catch up on our lives."

Grace couldn't help the smile that slipped across her face. Jon saw it, and added his to it. "Okay?"

"Sure, okay." She ducked her head, fumbled for the doorknob behind her, and finally spilled into air that wasn't filled with the delectable scent of sawdust and cotton and all things delightfully Jon.

* * *

By the time lunch came and went, the cookies baked and eaten, and three batches of cupcakes had been mixed, baked, frosted, and taken around for samples, Grace felt ready to drop. She hadn't worked this hard since opening her own shop.

She loved the work though. Realized she'd missed it these past months as she closed things up, sold her lease, and moved to the Texas Panhandle.

"So, we've got the three types of brownies." Heidi bent over a list at the counter while Kelly washed dishes. Chelsea had left an hour ago to tend to her children, and Grace slid onto the barstool next to Heidi.

"I can do a blonde brownie too," Grace said. "And a key lime bar. That will give you five bar options."

Heidi added them to the list. "That should be plenty, don't you think?"

"With cookies and cupcakes, I definitely think so. Remember, it's a bakery. You'll be doing breads and pies too."

Heidi nodded, a worried expression crossing her face. She sucked her bottom lip into her mouth and bit it as she took notes. "So you'll be doing all the sweet stuff. And I'll do the breads. You said maybe five varieties per day?"

"Right," Grace said. "We'll do a pie of the day too. It'll make the workflow easier. Specific cupcake flavors too. And some staples. For example, we'll always have these brownies and cookies. And you'll always make white, wheat, and sourdough bread. The other two can rotate. That kind of thing."

Heidi's pencil flew across the page. "Okay, yes," she said. "All right." She put down her pencil. "It's been so long since I went to school. What would I do without you? I'm so glad Chelsea called you."

Grace smiled at Heidi, a kind woman who had given a lot to others over the years, if Chelsea was to be believed. And Grace believed her. "Me too, Heidi." She stretched her arm over Heidi's shoulders and gave her a side hug. "We'll get everything figured out. We have almost three months before you open."

Footsteps came down the hall, and Grace glanced up in time to see Jon emerge.

"Hey, Jon," Kelly said easily. "Enjoy your day off?"

"Smelled so good up here, I almost went mad." He gave her a playful grin. "Other than that, it was just fine."

She laughed and pointed to the fridge. "Not cookin' tonight. But there's some of that beef and broccoli left over from last night."

He shook his head, and panic poured through Grace. Would he announce they were going out? What would Heidi think then?

Grace wasn't sure why she cared. She was an adult —almost twenty-seven years old. She could go to dinner with whomever she liked, Jon included.

"I'm goin' into town for dinner," he said, his eye catching hers.

"Ooh, do you have a date?" Kelly asked, more interested than Grace thought she ought to be. But she'd learned that Brett and Jon had been living in the basement for going on four months, and she had no idea if Kelly had been trying to set Jon up or not.

"Sure do," Jon said, puffing out his already impressive chest. "And I didn't need your help this time, ma'am."

"Ma'am?" Kelly abandoned her work and stared at him. "Who is it?"

"Someone special," he said, stepping toward the door. "And I'm gonna be late, Miss Nosy."

"Jon," Kelly called after him. "Who is it?"

"I better go too," Grace said so she could walk out with Jon.

"See you tomorrow, dear," Heidi said absently, her attention back on her list. "Was eight o'clock okay?"

"Totally fine," Grace confirmed before she followed a laughing Jon out the door and onto the deck. She'd whip up the blondies and key lime bars before she came out to the ranch in the morning. She'd certainly have time.

She made it to the lawn and started toward where she'd parked her car, Jon at her side. "Thanks for not saying anything about...." Grace trailed off, not quite sure how to finish.

His hand brushed hers, and fire licked up her arm. Another brush, and he held on this time. "I know how to keep important things to myself," he said.

"Oh, am I important?" Grace teased.

He squeezed her hand. "You were once. I'm interested in seeing if you can be again." He paused, making her stall too. "Can we do that, Gracie? See if this could be our second chance?"

Warmth filled Grace from top to bottom from the

kindness in his tone, the hope etched around his eyes. She reached up and pulled his cowboy hat down an inch or two. "Sounds good to me, *cowboy*."

He growled, the sound playful and sexy, and Grace giggled as she danced away from him. "When did you start wearing a cowboy hat anyway?"

"'Bout the time I came to Texas, I reckon. The summers here are brutal. The ball cap wasn't cutting it."

Grace floated toward her car, her new life in Three Rivers brighter than ever, despite the darkness she'd brought with her from Dallas.

* * *

Jon's nerves seemed frayed, like he'd stuck them in a blender on high. He almost turned around and went back to the ranch twice. But the thought of spending the evening hungry and with only Brett for company made his fingers tighten on the steering wheel.

He just couldn't believe Grace had walked right back into his life. He'd barely started to get to know her before her family moved, and he certainly didn't have much to offer her besides a nomadic lifestyle and days filled with long hours.

Happiness sang through him that she'd been able

to attend culinary school—something she'd told him she wanted to do the very first time they'd met. Well, she'd told the whole English class—he wasn't special— but he'd felt like she was speaking directly to him that day.

Jon also hadn't been on a date worth talking about in a while, despite Kelly's attempts at fixing him up with the single women in town. They'd been fine, nice, but not memorable. He wanted fireworks, electricity, excitement.

He'd felt all of that with Grace, then and now. "Doesn't mean you're gonna get married," he muttered to himself as he came to a stop behind her. He'd told her to choose where she wanted to go; he'd follow her.

She turned right, and his stomach tightened. There were only two restaurants to the right, and neither of them appealed to him. He just didn't understand how anyone could think kimchi tasted good. Or at least okay. In his mind, sour cabbage should be given to hogs. In fact, he *had* fed it to hogs in the past.

Thankfully, Grace drove past the Korean restaurant and pulled into the steakhouse. Donna's on Main Street was definitely superior, but at least Jon could get a burger here. Or maybe a steak sandwich.... His mind revolving around food, he forgot to obsess over possible dinner conversation topics or how he could kiss Grace after only a few hours of face-to-face time.

He got out of the car and joined her. "You've eaten here before?"

"Once," she said, peering up at him. "Is this okay? You'd prefer somewhere else."

"This is fine, Gracie Lou."

She made a face and moaned. "I'm okay with Gracie, I guess, but not Gracie Lou."

"Really?" He held the door open for her, his body reacting when hers moved closer, brushed by him, and entered the restaurant. "But you used to like—" He silenced himself before he could bring up the memories she'd rather forget. But how could she forget that he'd called her Gracie Lou right before he'd kissed her for the first time?

Back then, she'd blushed and ducked her chin, just like she had in the basement when she'd brought him the brownies.

His stomach, now a cold stone, weighed him down as the hostess led them to a booth and placed menus in front of them.

"I'm just Grace now." She ignored her menu and added a one-shouldered shrug to her statement. "I don't know why. Just feels like me."

"Just Grace it is." But Jon secretly mourned the loss of Gracie without letting any emotion bleed onto his face. "So you went to New York City. Tell me about that."

Her face lit up and she put her elbows on the table as she leaned forward. She began to talk about creams and puddings and something called a ganache. Jon wasn't exactly sure what she was talking about, but he just liked listening to the sound of her voice. Even after they'd finished eating and he'd given her a hug good-bye and driven back to the ranch, the sweet timbre of her voice rang in his ears.

That was when he knew he was in trouble. After all, he didn't live in Three Rivers and Grace had just moved to town.

Chapter Three

Grace went through the drive-through to get her daily fix of caffeine. A pan of blondies and a jelly roll pan of key lime bars rode in the backseat, the smell mixing with her dark roast coffee and making her mouth water.

She again enjoyed the leisurely drive out to the ranch—until she saw the sign and turned onto the dirt road. Then the coffee she'd finished seemed to turn to tar in her stomach. She'd had a great time with Jon the previous night—he'd starred in her dreams as the heroic cowboy carpenter that would sweep her away to live a fantastic life together—and the thought of seeing him again made her...nervous.

Once around the bend, the new construction came into view. Three men worked on the roof, and Grace identified Jon easily. His tall frame straightened, his gaze fixed on her car. He smiled and lifted his hand in a welcome wave. She did the same, trying not to frantically wave her hand like an excited puppy's tail.

She couldn't be *that* obvious. She'd arrived early again, and she removed the baked goods she'd prepared that morning and balanced them on the roof of her car. She put a few of each kind on two of the paper plates she'd brought and headed for the construction site.

This isn't too obvious, is it? she wondered as she tromped through the dust. She assured herself that she'd also planned to take some over to Courage Reins, where the brownies had been well received yesterday. The owner, Pete Marshall, had told her to come back any time with any kind of sweet. When Grace had mentioned his reaction to Chelsea, she'd laughed and said, "I have him on a strict diet right now. His blood sugar is out of control."

She'd just have to keep this early-morning treat a little secret. "Hey," she called up to the boys on the roof. "I have key lime bars and blondies." She glanced around for a place to set the plate. "Should I—?"

"We'll come down," a dark-haired man with a full beard called. She'd met Brett yesterday, and he didn't say a whole lot, which unsettled her. The quiet ones always did.

He greeted her first and took one of each bar. He'd eaten his whole key lime bar before the other two men appeared. "This is fantastic, Miss Grace," he said. "My wife would love these."

Jon and another man, Luis, selected their treats too. Grace wasn't sure what to do. Say "Great, enjoy," and walk away? She should. Anyone else probably would. But she wanted to breathe in the clean, minty scent of Jon's aftershave and press her cheek to his chest to feel his pulse bump against her skin.

"Morning," she said to him as Luis moved away to find a spot of shade.

With his mouth full, he simply nodded. Once he swallowed, he said, "Mornin', Miss Grace."

She indicated the blondie. "You like it?"

He considered it. "It's great, yeah."

Her heart fell to the dirt and rebounded back to her chest like a yo-yo. "You don't like it?"

He put the rest of the bar in his mouth—he obviously liked it. That, or he was really hungry. Or maybe he was part goat and would eat anything. "I think it's great," he said. "I just like chocolate brownies better."

"Yeah, I get that." She flashed him a grateful smile. "Chocolate is the way to go."

"So this is...?"

"Key lime bar," she said. "It's tart and sweet."

He cocked one eyebrow at the dessert and then at her before taking a bite. He moaned and his beautiful eyes closed. "Gracie, you're a genius in the kitchen."

Grace's chest swelled with pride. "Thank you, Jon." She glanced over her shoulder as a couple of trucks came around the bend and pulled into the Courage Reins parking lot. "Well, I better get these over to the people across the street."

Jon's intense stare made her blush, though she wasn't sure why. "All right then."

Grace felt like he was dismissing her, because it wasn't the reaction she wanted. She wanted him to ask her to stay just another minute, or touch her hand before she left, or ask her to come back at lunchtime so he could see her again.

Something tortured passed through his expression before he turned away. "Thanks for the treats, Grace."

"Yeah, thanks Grace," Brett called, and Luis lifted his hand in gratitude. As Jon moved away, another snag of disappointment caught behind Grace's lungs. She turned and hurried across the street, so she wouldn't have to be rejected by him so openly and completely in front of other people.

Her pride had been punched, and she tried to eradicate the pinch in her chest before pushing through the door of Courage Reins. The receptionist glanced up and then nearly toppled his chair as he stood and came around the counter.

"Miss Grace, welcome." Reese beamed at her, and her wounded pride lifted a little bit. "What do you have for us today?" He stopped and leaned against the counter as Pete poked his head out of the conference room.

"I am so happy Heidi is opening a bakery," he said, a grin gracing his strong features.

She smiled at the cowboys. "Key lime bars and blondies." She passed the plate to Reese, who set it on the counter. "I have more in the car. I just need a couple for Heidi and the other women."

"I'll help you get them," Reese said. He followed her back to the car, his injured leg dragging a little bit. "My wife will be upset she stayed home today."

"Sneak one behind the counter," Grace said.

"Pete'll be able to sniff that thing out by lunch." Reese chuckled. "The lieutenant has the nose of a hound dog."

"I can take it to her on my way home," Grace offered. "Is she not feeling well today?"

A grave look of sadness etched itself across Reese's face. "She's...okay. It's...."

"Never mind," Grace said quickly. She'd only met Reese and his wife Carly a couple of times at church and their personal lives were none of her business. She busied herself with cutting the bars and sliding them onto another paper plate.

"Our adoption fell through," Reese blurted. "Carly spoke to the birth mother last night, and she's...dealing with the loss today."

Grace's muscles tightened and her motions stalled. "Oh, I'm so sorry." She put her hand on Reese's arm. "I didn't know you were trying to adopt."

Anger and hope and regret passed across his face. "Have been for a while." He took a deep breath. "It's okay. I have faith in the Lord. I believe He'll give us a baby when the time is right."

Grace marveled at the strength in him. "And Carly? She believes that too?"

"She does," he murmured as he took the plate of goodies from her. "We just all deal with setbacks in different ways, even if we have faith. Right?"

Grace smiled at him. "Of course, right." She thought about her own losses, the enormous weight of debt she carried on her slim shoulders. She had faith things would work out—just as surely as Carly did— but sometimes seeing the light through the darkness was more difficult than anticipated. Grace knew that better than most.

"Thank you, Miss Grace." Reese tipped his cowboy hat and started across the street. She watched him go, a silent prayer for him and Carly floating through her mind. It felt good to pray for someone else for a change—she'd spent so many months praying for herself, for her cupcakery, for what *she* wanted that she'd somewhat forgotten that others experienced pain and trials too.

She inhaled deeply, taking the fresh scent of ranch air in through her nose to clear her head. *Thank you for bringing me to Three Rivers.* The peace she felt here lifted the weight of the money she owed and the failure she felt so keenly.

Chelsea emerged from the front door of her house, one baby strapped to her body and her toddler's hand in hers. Grace smiled in their direction and collected the remaining treats before glancing toward the construction site.

She wished Jon would be standing on the roof, watching her. But he wasn't. He was bent over, his focus only on his work. Grace sighed, not sure why she'd expected him to act any different, and headed into the house for another day of baking.

Jon HATED the disappointment he'd caught on Grace's face. He'd wanted to hold her, breathe her in, brush his lips along her cheek, but he couldn't. Not in mixed company, and he probably shouldn't at all if he didn't have plans for something more long-term. He didn't want another three-month relationship with Grace. He'd already done that, and been unsatisfied.

With every pulse of the staple gun, a question burst into his mind. *So what do you want to do?*

He placed another tar shingle and pressed the stapler flush against it. *Staple, staple.*

Move to Three Rivers permanently?

What would you even do here?

Another shingle. Another couple of staples.

Is there a construction firm here?

Maybe you could start your own. And do what?

He reached for another stack of shingles, the heat even this early in the morning almost unbearable. But it wasn't really. The temperature had skyrocketed since Grace had shown up with those treats, wearing a pair of skinny jeans and a blue flowered tank top.

The shingle made a slapping sound against the roof as he threw it down. He positioned it, the muscles in his back stretching as he placed the stapler along the edge. *Staple, staple, staple.*

Build sheds?

Are there housing developments here?

Enough home improvement jobs?

As the shingles went down in even rows and the minutes passed, Jon tormented himself. By the time

Brett called to him to come down to get out of the sun and get a drink, Jon hadn't arrived at a solution yet.

Maybe there wasn't a solution. Maybe he should accept Grace's goodies whenever she brought them, mind his own business, and go back to Oklahoma City when the job ended, just like he'd been planning.

He'd certainly never looked at Three Rivers as a permanent place to put down roots. The very thought actually made him physically ill, and he stumbled on the ladder. Brett lurched forward to help him, knocking Jon's hat off.

"I'm okay," Jon said. "I'm fine."

"Come get a drink now." Brett's commanding tone wasn't lost on Jon, and he actually appreciated it. He'd known Brett since childhood, watched him get married and go off to war, had been there when he'd come home the first time, and the second, and the third.

He obeyed Brett, relishing the icy water as it touched his tongue and flowed down his throat. But he knew he wasn't dehydrated, at least not enough to make him stumble down a ladder, something he'd navigated easily for decades.

He refused to look toward the homestead, instead closing his eyes and breathing deep.

"Eat this."

He opened his eyes to Brett holding a Snickers bar toward him.

"I'm fine."

"Eat it." He shook the candy bar, the plastic wrapper rattling.

Jon glared as he took the bar and unwrapped it. "Commander, it's not the heat."

Brett cocked his head and appraised him in that calculating way all Army men had. Jon had briefly considered following his friend into the Army, but he'd chosen the Marines instead.

"What is it then?" Brett asked.

The water he'd drunk sloshed against his stomach walls. "It's Grace Lewis."

Brett's gaze wandered to the homestead, and Jon could practically see Brett's wheels spinning. "That's Grace Lewis? *The* Grace Lewis? The one you liked in high school?"

Jon pressed his mouth into a thin line and nodded.

"Didn't you take her to homecoming?"

"Yep."

"She moved...." Brett reached up and rubbed his beard, his eyes thoughtful. "Funny how you and her ended up here at the same time, all these years later."

"We went to dinner last night."

Brett switched his shrewd gaze to Jon. "Oh, yeah?"

"Yeah."

"And?"

Jon filled his cup from the orange cooler again,

taking a minute to get away from Brett's blazing eyes. "I like her, okay? But...." He looked out over the endless horizon, the undulating fields, imagining he could see the little town of Three Rivers, where he'd never wanted to come.

He turned back to Brett. "But she just moved here to help Heidi open her bakery, and well, I threw a fit about even coming here for a few months to work."

Brett started nodding before Jon finished speaking. "What do you have lined up after this?"

Jon didn't want to say "nothing," but he did anyway.

Brett gave him the courtesy of thinking for several minutes while Jon munched on the candy bar. He did feel new life entering his bloodstream from the sugar, and he took off his cowboy hat and wiped his forehead.

"Maybe God brought you here to reconnect," Brett finally said.

Jon had already entertained that idea, and told Brett so.

He held up his hands. "Okay, I won't counsel you. I'm just sayin' that it's not the first time the Lord has used Three Rivers to help two people reconnect." He stacked his cup on the top of the orange cooler, whistled for Luis, who had wandered out onto the plains, and started up the ladder to resume work on the roof.

Jon took a few extra minutes in the shade, contemplating how he felt and what Brett had said. He mulled over possibilities for a long-term relationship with Grace, but before he could truly come up with one viable option, the woman who'd been tormenting his every waking thought for the past twenty-four hours came walking toward him.

Chapter Four

Grace had begged Heidi to wait until lunch—
when all the cowhands would come to the
house anyway—to allow samples of the goods they'd
baked that morning. She didn't mind traipsing all over
the ranch—it was one way to get in her steps for the
day—but she didn't want to face Jon again until they
could be alone.

Yet there he stood, alone, in the shadowy doorway
of the barn he'd been working on all morning. Yes,
she'd taken a peek here and there in between batches
of sourdough and honey wheat, and while the
cupcakes baked, she'd brainstormed staple flavors of
frostings and fillings while she stood at the wide wall of
windows in the kitchen.

Jon had been on the roof all morning, his focus

admirable, his work ethic second-to-none. Why, oh why, had Heidi timed her delivery of samples with his morning break?

"Hey," she said as she approached with a tray of her cupcakes clutched in her hands. She really wanted him to like them, as if his opinion alone could resurrect her failed business in Dallas.

"Salted caramel chocolate," she said indicating the cupcakes on her left with her chin. "And peanut butter chocolate chip. Oh, and Heidi sent samples of her bread too. Sourdough and honey wheat. She says she'll be making sandwiches out of the bread at noon. Everyone is welcome to come eat lunch at the homestead."

Jon patted his flat stomach. "I just ate."

Her spirits deflated. "I made the cupcakes. You like chocolate." She hated that the desperation in her voice had sounded so loudly.

"Look, Grace—"

"Okay," she said loudly as she moved to the ladder. "Boys, there are cupcakes here."

It took less than ten seconds for Brett to shimmy down the ladder. He took one of the peanut butter cupcakes Grace had presented him with, and the look of pure bliss on his face brought a smile to Grace's face.

"Lunch at noon," she told him and Luis before turning toward the equine therapy center. Kelly and

Chelsea had spent the bulk of the morning talking about Pete and his program, who they worked with, and how Pete needed more cowhands to help because his clientele had expanded so much.

"Grace, wait."

She turned at the plea in Jon's voice, but she didn't give him the satisfaction of a verbal answer. Instead, she cocked her hip and waited.

"I want one of those caramel ones."

She made him to come to her, her pulse speeding with every step he took. He selected the smallest of the cupcakes, though they all seemed to be the same size. His eyes didn't leave hers as he took a bite, the whipped cream smearing across his upper lip. Her gaze dropped to his mouth, and everything inside her wanted to lean closer and lick the cream from his lips.

Startled at the strong urge, she stepped back. "Enjoy." She turned before he could see the burning in her face.

"Grace, I don't live in Three Rivers."

A few seconds passed before his words registered in her ears. A few more for her to face him again and set the tray of goodies on the ground, her movement slow and jerky at the same time. "Okay," she said to the top of his cowboy hat, as he'd ducked his head to finish his cupcake.

He licked his fingers and met her eye. "I don't live here, and I don't...." He exhaled and looked away.

"You're not interested," Grace said. "It's okay, Jon. Really." Her heart would recover. He'd only been in her life for one day. Surely it wouldn't take that long to get over him. Certainly not as long as last time. She started to move away again.

"Wait, what?" His fingers landed on her bare upper arm, sending electricity to her fingertips and into her forehead. "Of course I'm interested." His hand slid down her arm and into hers. "I'm really interested in *you*. I'm not interested in living in Three Rivers."

Ah, so there it sat. She blinked at him, not quite sure which part of what he'd said to process first. The fact that he was interested in her? Or that he'd been cold and distant that morning to deliberately push her away because he wasn't a permanent resident of the town where she now lived?

"I—How long will you be here?" She examined the worksite behind him as if the wood could tell her when the barn would be finished.

"Through Christmas probably. I was hopin' to be home for the holidays, actually." He ran his free hand up the back of his neck, disturbing his hat the slightest bit. "I'm sorry about this morning. I don't know if you noticed, but—"

"I noticed." She squeezed his fingers. "And it's

okay. We don't have to get married by Christmas." She smiled up at him, leaning into his body a little bit more and taking his other hand with hers. "Right?"

Heat and desire ran through his eyes as he gazed down on her. She lost herself to the chemistry between them, the current that connected him to her, the shelter of his cowboy hat as he dipped his face closer to hers.

For one breathtaking moment, she thought he'd kiss her right then. Her lips tingled in anticipation of meeting his again. Sure, she'd kissed him before, but it had been a long time and she couldn't quite remember the taste of him, the shape of his mouth against hers. And she wanted to.

His lips skated across her cheek, landing in the hollow just below her ear. "So, what are we gonna do?"

"Do?" She mimicked his hushed tone, her hands sliding up his impressive biceps to hold onto his shoulders. His kiss, though it hadn't landed on her lips, had rendered her weak.

"It's only a few weeks until Christmas."

"It's two and a half months until Christmas, Jon." She giggled, the sound fading into a gasp as his breath coasted across her skin.

"It's too soon," he whispered.

Something clattered above them, and Grace jumped out of Jon's arms, startled and embarrassed at the same time.

"Jon?" Brett called. "Oh, there you are. You comin'?"

Grace had the feeling that Brett had seen their embrace and done his best to spare them the embarrassment of catching them.

"Yeah." Jon didn't look away from her. "I'm comin'."

"See you at lunch."

He took a couple of steps backward and lifted his hand in farewell, before turning and striding toward the ladder. She watched him haul his tall, muscular frame up the rungs and disappear onto the roof.

With giddiness galloping through her veins, a sense of uncertainty also tainted her thoughts.

A lot can happen in two and a half months, she told herself as she went to deliver more samples.

JON ADORED EVERYTHING Grace had a hand in creating. The bread was light and fluffy on Tuesday during lunch. The cupcakes on Wednesday possessed just the right balance of sweetness and saltiness and savory-ness. The piecrust on Thursday melted in his mouth. By Friday morning, everything in Jon felt wound tight.

He woke before his alarm, the first time in months,

with Grace swimming in his head. The smell of her perfume teased him though it wasn't present. The silkiness of her skin made his fingers itch. The softness of her neck called to him.

He rose, as frustrated with himself as with the situation. He wanted to kiss her more than he wanted to breathe. But he also didn't want to kiss her and start something he couldn't finish. *Not fair, not fair*, floated through his mind. He didn't want to string her along for the next two months only to leave town when the job was done but the relationship wasn't.

Why start a relationship? he asked himself as he stepped into the shower. He'd been asking himself the same question for days. He still hadn't found an answer. With a start that made him slip, he realized maybe he should've been asking a different question.

Why *not* start a relationship?

People had long-distance relationships all the time. And Oklahoma City wasn't that far from Three Rivers. And she'd be working a lot anyway, getting the bakery started.

With a lighter heart and muscles that weren't as tight as springs, he headed out to the patio, almost tripping over Grace as he came face-to-face with her sittin' in the very rocking chair where he'd been aiming to enjoy his morning coffee. The hot liquid sloshed over the lip of the mug and onto the back of his hand.

"Grace," he gasped. He switched the mug to his other hand and licked the coffee from his hand. "Just a sec." He returned to the kitchen and ran cold water over his burning hand. It cooled in only a few seconds —long enough for her to stand and lean in the doorway, effectively blocking his escape from the basement.

Behind him, Brett's alarm went off, and Jon heard the man start to stir. "What are you doin' here so early?"

"This isn't that early," she said by way of answer.

"It's barely six-thirty." He pointed to the coffee pot. "You want some?"

She lifted a travel cup. "Brought my own."

Jon felt trapped, unsure of why she was here and how he could get outside to the fresh air faster. He stepped toward her, taking in the magnificence of her long legs and accentuated curves as she leaned her shoulders into the doorframe. "Want to sit out here?"

She backed out of the doorway and he stepped past her. "You can have the rocker." He took a position on the low wall next to the steps and took a sip of his coffee. "So if this isn't early, what is?"

Collapsing into the rocking chair, she let out a sigh and sipped her own coffee. "My internal alarm goes off at three a.m. Side-effect of pastry school." She leaned her head back and closed her eyes. Jon watched her, his gaze sweeping over the gentle column of her neck, her shoulders. The white top she wore was gauzy and see-through to the aqua tank underneath. Jon's leg muscles bunched and he didn't dare lift his coffee mug to his mouth for fear he wouldn't be able to swallow.

"Did you make anything delicious this morning?" he asked, though she'd brought herself and she was certainly delectable enough.

"No, I took a long bath and read a book this morning." She opened her eyes, smiled, and lifted that lucky coffee mug to her mouth. Jon had never wanted to be an inanimate object so badly.

He hadn't asked her to dinner again. He hadn't made the mistake of holding her in plain sight again. He hadn't done more than get her number and text her for hours after he finished working each afternoon. He wasn't sure why. Indecision, probably. After all, Jon was the king of indecision.

"You want to go to church with me on Sunday?" she asked.

He raised his eyes to her, but she continued to rock in the chair as if asleep. "Sure." Kicking a grin in her direction, he added, "Doesn't start until eleven. Think you can stay awake that long, sleepyhead?"

Her eyes opened, but they didn't focus for a few minutes. When she caught him smiling at her, she rolled her eyes. "Maybe. Maybe not. Could be an adventure."

"I could use a little adventure."

"I'll say. The most exciting thing you do is text past ten p.m."

A flash of guilt stole through him. "I didn't know you got up at three a.m.," he protested. "In fact, I don't know anyone who gets up that early. It's insane."

She yawned. "It's so quiet here."

"I'll stop talking so you can go back to sleep." He watched her eyes drift closed again. "Honest, Gracie, I wouldn't have texted so late if I'd known you got up so early."

She smiled in his general direction without opening her eyes. "It's okay. You can make it up to me by taking me to the picnic after church. I heard it's good."

The thought of being seen in public with a woman as beautiful and kind as Grace made his mouth feel like he'd been sucking on cotton balls. The coffee didn't help. "It is."

"Mm." She seemed to actually fall asleep right there on the patio, and Jon relaxed in a way he hadn't for the past five days. Just being with her, here, alone, felt comfortable. In every other situation, he'd felt like he was playing a part, acting. But when it was just him and her, he didn't need to be anyone but himself.

And for the second time in the past five days, Jon

knew he was in big trouble. Because Grace was making it harder and harder for him to leave Three Rivers.

* * *

JON HELD Grace's hand through the service, and while he gave her the opportunity to let go before they stepped out of the chapel, she didn't. In fact, she slid her hand up his arm to the crook of his elbow and held on tight. They strolled to the park along with families and other couples, Brett several paces ahead of them with Squire and Kelly and their kids.

He hadn't become friends with a whole lot of people in Three Rivers. He hadn't seen the need. He lived out at the ranch; he worked out at the ranch. The only time he even went to town was for groceries and to attend church. He'd gone to the picnic a few times, mostly with women Kelly had set him up with. A couple of them eyed him now, with the gorgeous Grace hanging on his arm.

She charmed everyone outgoing enough to approach her. She told them all the same story: she'd moved to town to help Heidi start her bakery. The mere mention of Heidi Ackerman made everyone smile and accept Grace—and by extension, Jon—with chuckles and "welcome, y'all"s.

To his surprise, Grace didn't put any desserts on

her plate. "You don't eat sweets on the weekend?" he asked as he picked up two chocolate chip cookies.

"Those aren't homemade," she hissed to him. "I'm picky." She took a cup of lemonade. "And if you must know, I do try to limit my sugar intake sometimes. Not all of us work out all day long for a living." The way her eyes swept the height of his body made a blush burst to life everywhere she looked.

He took the opportunity to once again admire her curves, though he tried to make it seem like this was the first time he'd noticed her body. "You look fine to me."

"Fine?" Her eyebrows went up with her voice. "You're *so* kind, Mister Carver. I know I have a few extra pounds on me. But you know what they say." She sashayed away a few steps.

Jon hurried to get his own cup of lemonade and follow her. "No, Grace, I have no idea what they say."

"Never trust a skinny chef." She flashed him a flirtatious smile as she sat at a picnic table no one had claimed yet. He sat across from her, thinking he wouldn't be able to control himself if he sat right next to her. The urge to hold her hand had him clenching his fists and the desire to kiss her drove all other thoughts from his mind.

He participated in the conversation with Brett and Squire and Pete, but he wasn't exactly sure what he'd said. He ate, but he didn't know how anything tasted. The picnic began to break up as some families left and others moved to play horseshoes or volleyball.

"You want to go for a walk?" he asked as he stood and collected their plates. "There's a path around the park, and over in that corner, there's a duck pond." He nodded to the farthest corner from the picnic tables.

"Sure." Grace stood too, and when Jon returned, she held hands with Julie, Pete's little three-year-old. "She wants to come."

Jon crouched in front of the little girl. "Oh, yeah? Want to feed the ducks?" The little girl stared at him with wide, serious eyes. "All right, then. Let's go."

They'd taken a few slow steps away when Chelsea said, "Julie, honey. You can't go."

"Mama—"

Chelsea shook her head. "No, Daddy's got to get back to check on the horses." She looked at Grace with an edge in her eye that Jon couldn't identify. "You said you'd help, remember?" She extended her hand toward her daughter. "Come on. We're going."

Julie looked like she might cry, but Grace bent down and said something to her, which caused the girl to release her hand and take her mother's instead.

Jon claimed Grace's other hand, squeezing it tightly as they stepped onto the path. The noise of the picnic faded the farther they walked, and Grace tilted her head back and looked into the bright autumn sky. "Tell me why you don't like it here."

He took a deep breath, his body filling with gratitude for his health, his job, his seemingly easy life. "I don't know."

She scoffed. "That's a cop-out. You know."

Jon half-appreciated her candor and was half-annoyed at her nosiness. He hadn't had anyone push him like this before. At least not for a long time.

"I'm more of a big-city type of guy," he said.

"You still in Oklahoma City?"

"My father's firm is there."

"Is it still your father's?"

"No."

"So you own it."

"Yeah."

"But you're not there." She finally turned her head to look at him. "How are you living here for this job?" He heard the "why" in the question too.

"I have a foreman and a floor manager who actually run the business," he explained. "I work on projects when I'm in town, if they need me. Otherwise, I take the jobs that are out of town. It's easier."

"Easier?"

Jon felt weary. He wished he had the strength and endurance of the tall trees that lined the path, effectively shading them and blocking this conversation from the rest of the world.

"Most of my men have families," he said. "It's harder for them to leave town. It's not hard for me."

"Even when you have to go somewhere you don't like?"

He nudged her with his hip. "You always this inquisitive?"

She paused and looked back down the path the way they'd come. "I am when I'm trying to find a solution to a problem."

His arms seemed to have a mind of their own as they wound around her waist and drew her closer to him. "Oh? What's the problem?"

"You leaving town." She looked right at him, open and honest and unassuming.

"That's a problem for you?" he teased, though a vein of seriousness rode underneath his playful tone.

She leaned into him and wrapped her hands around the back of his neck. "Oh, it's a big problem." She lifted onto her toes. "I'm going to kiss you now, okay? Is that going to be a problem for you?"

"Oh, yeah," he said, his tone turning deep and husky at the same time his pulse shot to the top of his skull. "It's gonna be a big problem."

Grace gripped the back of his cowboy hat in her

fingers and tilted it off his head. "You don't want me to?"

"Grace, kissing you is all I've thought about since I saw you strumming my guitar on the patio." He leaned down to meet her lips with his. A shiver shot down his spine with the first touch, and then he drew a breath and molded his mouth to hers for a deeper exploration of her lips.

"Definitely a *huge* problem," he whispered before kissing her again.

Chapter Five

Kissing Jon under the Texas trees felt more magical than Grace remembered. Of course, last time, she'd kissed him on her front porch after the homecoming dance. There wasn't a brightly shining sun or a whisper of a breeze through decades-old trees. Or the worry that one of them would leave town in two months.

She didn't want to complicate his life, but at the same time, she totally did. She wanted to kiss him in the middle of the night before she left for the bakery, and then have him wake her with a kiss when he got back from his construction project that night.

The strength of her ideas startled her a bit—enough for Jon to notice and break the kiss. She stood in the circle of his arms and pressed her cheek against his chest to find his heart hammering. She smiled to know she elicited such a response from such a strong man.

"So," she said. "We need to figure out what to do."

He stiffened the slightest bit. "Do we? Can't we just, I don't know, go to dinner and sit by each other at church and kiss by the duck pond every chance we get?"

Grace wanted to, and she sighed into him. "I don't think you get into town much. Seems like kissing at the duck pond is off the table."

His grip along her waist tightened. "I can make the drive."

She laughed at the sexy bite in his tone. "All right, handsome. Let's see if this pond is all you said it was." She slipped out of his arms at the same time she laced her fingers through his. They walked the circumference of the park, the conversation as easy as the fall breeze, but deep inside, Grace harbored worry.

Worry that Jon really meant what he'd said about pursuing a more casual relationship. Worry that Jon didn't want to commit. Worry that Jon wouldn't stay in town, even for her.

She'd just need to change his mind. Filled with determination—especially after he followed her home and kissed her so completely she couldn't think, or breathe, or stand—Grace decided to do everything she could to make him fall in love with Three Rivers.

If only she knew how.

* * *

"A HALLOWEEN PARTY?" Jon glanced up from the invitation Grace had given him. "I'm not dressin' up."

"It's not required." She pointed to the asterisk that said as much. "Heidi just wants to test out her baking on as many people as possible. She claims the cowhands will eat anything she gives them."

Over the past two weeks, Grace had streamlined the menu, the baking schedule, the entire process. And she wanted to experiment. See if she could make an entire bakery's worth of treats in one day and have them be edible. Have them be something people would pay for.

So, yes, the Halloween party had been her idea, though she was more than willing to let Heidi play hostess.

"It's at my house," Grace said. "Since Heidi's condo is too small to hold as many people as she thinks will come."

Jon cocked one eyebrow at her. "You realize the whole town will come."

Grace gave him her best smile. "We're counting on it. If they taste the treats and like them, they'll be more likely to come and pay when we open."

"They'll come no matter what," he mumbled as he swung his head away from her.

"What does that mean?" A sick feeling took root in Grace's stomach.

"It means that Heidi Ackerman is Three Rivers royalty. If she opens a bakery in town, people will come just because it's her."

Grace swallowed down a fresh wave of bitterness, because what he'd said was true. "Well, it's not Heidi's baking."

"Doesn't matter," Jon said. "It has her name on it."

As if the pressure Grace carried wasn't heavy enough. "I need you to come."

He focused on her again. "You *need* me to come?" His eyes sharpened, taking on a dangerous edge she found exciting. So exciting that a grin formed on her face.

"I want you to come, and yes, I need you to come. I...I don't want to be the only one there without someone they know."

"You know people."

"I know three people. And they'll all have husbands and children and other friends there. So I need a friend there too."

He inched closer to her. "A friend?"

Grace shrugged one shoulder. "Sure. We're friends."

He growled, one hand sweeping around her waist in a smooth movement. "No, we're not friends." He touched his lips to her shoulder and a tremor quaked in her center.

"Can I call you my boyfriend, then?" She cocked her head as he stiffened. "I guess not. That has the word friend in it, and we're not friends." She smirked at him, but he stared at her without any hint of amusement.

He brought his mouth to hers with all the urgency of a tropical storm, and she got swept up in the cool touch of his lips, the sweet taste of his tongue, the gentle pressure on her back. When he drew back, he whispered, "Fine, you can call me your boyfriend."

She exhaled, trying to will strength back into her limbs before he released her. "And you'll come to the party?"

"Yeah, all right. I'll come to the party."

She stepped away and pulled the hem of her shirt down to straighten it. "I'm glad we've established some things today." She flounced away while he fisted the Halloween party invitation.

* * *

A week later, Jon showed up at Grace's house a couple of hours before the party began. He pulled all the way into her open garage, like she'd instructed him to, put his truck in park, and sat in it. Parking here would mean he couldn't leave until the very end of the party. After everyone else had left. Part of him rejoiced at being able to spend so much time with Grace. The other part had been dying for seven solid days.

Because Jon didn't go to parties. Certainly not Halloween parties. He certainly saw nothing worth celebrating about the holiday.

Movement caught his peripheral vision and he reached to unbuckle his seatbelt. "Hey," he called to Grace as he got out of his truck. "I brought the dry ice."

"Perfect." She met him at the tailgate with a rolling cooler. "You need this?"

He pulled the cooler full of dry ice from the truck bed. "No, I think I got it."

"Okay, let's put it in the kitchen. Most of the party will be in the backyard, but I've never trusted coolers to keep things cold."

Jon chuckled as he followed her into her house. He'd never been inside, because they either went out after he finished working, or she stayed out at the ranch for the evening, or he followed her home and kissed her pressed up against her front door.

He kicked the door closed behind him and put the cooler where she indicated he should. Then he took her in his arms and kissed her, his nerves settling and his stomach swooping with her eager response. "I've missed you the last couple of days," he murmured into her hair as he rubbed slow circles on her back.

"Mm, that's nice to hear." She pulled back and grinned at him. "Now come on. You promised to help and well, this isn't exactly helping."

"It's not?"

"Not the kind of help I need right now." She handed him a stack of serving trays and indicated a row of folding tables that had been set up in her backyard. "Put these trays on those tables."

"Yes, ma'am." He allowed her to boss him around, putting brownies on some trays, and cookies on another, and tarts on still more. By the time Heidi arrived, Jon thought Grace had surely done everything worth doing.

But Heidi brought in a basket filled with black and orange decorations, and she and Grace set about placing and adjusting and fixing every witch and each skeleton and all the bats until they were exactly right.

Jon helped at first, but when he caught Grace moving a cauldron he'd placed too close to the edge of the table, he took to carrying things from the house to the yard until the women declared things done.

By then, Chelsea and her family had arrived, along with Kelly and her family. Garth Ahlstrom, the foreman at Three Rivers Ranch, pulled in just as Jon closed Heidi's trunk and pocketed her keys.

He exchanged a hello with the foreman and his wife, a sharp stab of unexpected longing knifing him between the ribs as Garth put his son on his shoulders and headed through the garage. Jon stood stock still, staring after them, unsure as to what he was feeling and why. He'd never thought much about having a family. Never envisioned himself as married. Never even considered being a dad.

But now...his gaze wandered to the glowing square of a window in Grace's house, and he thought he'd like to be a family with her.

Anger accompanied the thought. *So what?* he asked himself—and God—with an edge of fury in the question.

"I'm not moving here," he vowed as he marched through the garage and into Grace's house. "I'm not."

Jon MANAGED to act his way through the party. He mingled and mixed and played games and ate more than a man should be able to consume. He held Grace's hand, and kept his arm around her waist, and pressed his lips to her temple. If anyone had any doubt about the status of his relationship with her before the party, they certainly wouldn't after.

The last of the partiers finally departed, leaving Grace and Jon with Heidi. Her husband had been smart and driven a separate car.

"Feedback was amazing, Grace." Heidi beamed at her. "I think the recipes we used today are the ones we should go with."

"I still want to try something different with that pumpkin pie tart."

"That will be a seasonal item anyway." Heidi's joviality faded.

Grace sighed and her eyes closed in a long blink. Jon knew she didn't stay up until eleven p.m., and he wondered if she'd be able to sleep past three tonight. "You're right. I'll tweak it as we go."

"Thank you, Grace." She picked up one basket of décor.

"Let me help you, ma'am." Jon collected a box of empty trays, which had held loaves of bread when she'd arrived. It took him a couple of trips, but he got everything out to her car and Heidi on her way in just a few minutes.

When he returned to the house, he found Grace fast asleep, her head cradled in her arms on the dining room table. He paused and watched her, the gentle rise of her upper back as she breathed in and out bringing a smile to his face.

He stepped toward her and crouched. "Grace," he said, but she didn't stir. For the first time—the first real time—he considered relocating to Three Rivers. He brushed her hair off the side of her face, the touch as electrifying as it was soft.

"I don't know if I can do it, Gracie," he whispered. "I really don't like small towns."

She sighed, and he tried to wake her again, this time succeeding as her eyes flew open. He soothed her by rubbing his hand up and down her arm. "Hey, you should go to bed before falling asleep."

She gave him a bleary smile, he helped her stand, and she leaned into him, her eyes already closed again. "Thanks for your help, Jon."

"Anytime, Gracie Lou." She didn't protest at the use of her nickname, simply tilted her head back and stretched up to kiss him good-night. He obliged, a river of guilt flowing through him. He shouldn't kiss her, lead her on, feel things for her when he was planning on leaving by Christmas.

Chapter Six

Grace leaned in the garage doorway and watched Jon back out of her driveway. She closed the garage door, the rumbling sound matching the quaking in her stomach.

"He's not going to stay," she said as the echoes of sound rattled around the garage. "You heard him." She turned, let the door fall closed, and locked it. She wasn't sure what she'd hoped Jon would do when she pretended to stay asleep when he tried to wake her. Kiss her like Sleeping Beauty? Declare his undying love for her when he thought she couldn't hear?

She shook her head, the danger of crying very real and very close. She certainly hadn't expected him to whisper that he didn't think he could stay in town. She'd stirred the next time he said her name, and she couldn't help kissing him good-bye. She didn't want to have a hard conversation near midnight, when her brain wasn't operational and her heart felt like it had been punctured by a coil of barbed wire.

A tear fell and Grace swiped it away. Would she ever feel successful? Her failed cupcakery hung over her like a thundercloud, and she couldn't hold back the waterworks this time.

After a good cry and a long shower, Grace took a steeling breath and squared her shoulders. She'd just do here what she'd had to do to get into pastry school. Try, try again. She'd dreamed of attending culinary school in New York City, and it had taken three attempts before she'd gotten in.

Maybe it'll just take a third time with Jon too. She pulled on pajamas, brushed out her hair, and fell into bed, exhausted. But she didn't want to break-up with him now and hope for a third chance meeting in the future.

Help me understand, she prayed. At once, a sense of calmness filled her, and she knew she needed to trust in the Lord's timing. She'd done it before with culinary school. With her cupcakery—although she'd lost her first shop in Dallas, Grace knew it was only a matter of timing before she'd own another bakery.

She'd just have to trust God regarding Jon, too.

* * *

Rain came with November, and Grace spent days inside, baking. Since Halloween and tasting her treats, the townspeople had been calling Grace and placing custom orders. With the bakery's storefront unavailable, she fielded the calls, managed the payments, and either did the baking herself or called Heidi to get the orders filled.

At first it was a birthday cake for a five-year-old's party. But by the third week, with Thanksgiving around the weekend, Grace found her phone ringing while she was on it.

She hung up with Amy Garrison, who had just ordered a half-dozen pies for her family's celebration the following week. Before she checked her messages, she dialed Heidi.

"Hello, dear. How's the baking going?"

"We have a bit of a problem," Grace started.

Heidi sighed. "What is it now?" Though she sounded tired, she didn't show signs of frustration. Grace admired her for her baking ability as well as her seemingly endless well of patience.

"Amy Garrison just ordered six pies for pickup on Wednesday." Her phone beeped, indicating another incoming call. "And my phone won't stop ringing. When do we cut off the orders?"

A few beats of silence had Grace picturing Heidi's

wise face contemplating her choices. "I'd hate to turn people away...."

"We already have sixty-six pies to deliver on Wednesday alone," Grace said. She could only bake four at a time. Heidi could cook an additional four. Without professional ovens and bakery-grade equipment, she'd allocated eight slots of baking time for her and Heidi for a total of sixty-four pies.

"You talked about an assembly line once," Heidi said. "Tell me more about that."

"Well, we make all the pie crusts and fillings—it helps that we're only offering three varieties this season —and send several uncooked but ready-to-bake pies out to the ranch. Chelsea and Kelly could probably bake... sixteen or so pies each." Grace felt bone-weary, and doing the math right now seemed impossible. But if Kelly and Chelsea could take two pie-baking slots each, they could bake sixteen pies in the morning and Grace could get them out to customers in the afternoon.

"So we can take on thirty-two more."

"Only thirty," Grace said firmly. "We're already over by two on our own lists."

"Thirty more then," Heidi said. "I guess I better get to the grocery store—and call Kelly and Chelsea."

Grace agreed and said good-bye. She answered the two messages she'd received and then updated the community Facebook page that only two dozen slots remained for pie orders. A thrill ran from the top of her head to the soles of her feet.

Though backed by the iconic Heidi Ackerman, her baking seemed to finally be striking the right notes with people. Her mother's voice snaked through her head, eliminating the rising euphoria.

You should've started in your own kitchen, Grace. Her mother had been trying to help, Grace knew. But that didn't make her words hurt any less. *You should've gotten established before trying a storefront.*

In the end, her mother had been right. Grace knew it. Her mother knew it. Everyone knew it. And many bakers did exactly what she'd tried to skip—what she was doing now with Heidi, baking from her home kitchen and trying to fill as many orders as possible.

The last pie slots sold out in the next half hour, and Grace headed over to Heidi's to make the master shopping list. Along the way, her phone chimed, igniting a sense of dread in her stomach as heavy as a brick. She didn't want to tell another person no. She'd put it on social media that they were full.

She didn't check the message until she'd parked at Heidi's. Jon had texted, and that sent Grace's stomach toward the heavens. She'd cooled their relationship over the past few weeks, citing her increased workload and the fact that she wasn't coming out to the ranch everyday. He still called, and texted, and took her to dinner sometimes. They sat next to one another at church, but she hadn't gone to another picnic, unable to face that park where she'd experienced the most perfect kiss of her life.

She hit call instead of texting him back. "What's up?" she asked as she got out of her car.

"Nothing's up. Just checking in." Like he was her father or something. Grace couldn't put her finger on why his statement annoyed her so much.

"Busy," she said. "About to meet with Heidi."

"I saw that you filled all your Thanksgiving pie slots."

"Yep." Had he called to talk about her baking? He'd never done that before, and Grace wondered if they'd hit a new low in their conversation.

"That's too bad," he said. "I was hoping you and I could enjoy a candlelit dinner for two, with a pecan pie for dessert."

She frowned at the flirty tone, at his suggestion that they'd spend Thanksgiving together. "I thought you were going home for Thanksgiving," she said. "You're not working, right?" She distinctly remembered him telling her that Brett wanted to be home to celebrate Thanksgiving with his family, who would then be coming to Texas until the project was finished. Jon had complained about having to move into one of the empty cowboy cabins and "fend for himself."

"Those plans fell through," he said.

"So I'm your second choice, is that it?" Her words flew from her mouth before she could tame them, and they had definite bite.

"Grace—"

She paused on the sidewalk at the base of Heidi's condo. "Look, Jon, I think we should just be done. We've been playing around, and it's been fun, but this isn't serious."

The silence on the other end of the line made her check her phone to make sure they hadn't been disconnected.

"It isn't?"

She almost rolled her eyes. "No, it isn't. You don't live here, and you have no intention of moving here. I do live here, and I'm happy here, and I'm hoping this bakery will be a huge success so I can keep living here."

"It's a—"

"Don't say it's a technicality," Grace said, her emotions spiraling up and out of control. She'd let him console her before, whisper words about how they didn't need to decide anything now. But not anymore. It was time to end this relationship, and she knew it.

"I'm sorry, Jon," she said. "I like you. Given enough time, I'm certain I could fall in love with you. But I'm not willing to do that over the phone or on the Internet." She took a deep breath to subdue the tears, but they wouldn't be tamed. "I have to go."

"Grace—" She heard him say as she hung up. In the next moment, a sob wrenched itself from her throat and tears painted her cheeks. She quieted herself quickly, taking a few precious minutes to make sure she was presentable before knocking on Heidi's door. The woman still saw her distress—or maybe she sensed it. She seemed to have a way of knowing things no one said or exhibited.

"Grace." She rushed forward. "What's wrong?"

Grace wanted to tell someone. She wanted support and encouragement from her friends, from Heidi. So she told her all about Jon.

* * *

JON STARED at his cell phone like it had morphed into a four-headed dog. Had Grace seriously just broken up with him? Over the phone?

You haven't really given her a reason to stay, he told himself as he stuffed the phone in his back pocket. Her accusation about being his second choice rang true. So true it hurt Jon's heart to think about.

She had come second these past two months. Second to the job. Second to his own desires. Second to who he'd spend Thanksgiving with. And now that his brother had given his parents a trip to New York for their thirty-fifth wedding anniversary, they wouldn't be in Oklahoma City next week.

Jon suddenly had nowhere to spend the holidays. He couldn't join the Ackerman's festivities, as Grace would be there.

"I'm heading back to get a drink," he yelled up to Brett, who called back to bring him a bottle of Gatorade. Jon stomped away from the construction site, angry at himself, at Texas, at the world.

What should I do? he asked as his fury faded, leaving only desperation and helplessness.

Make a decision, came into his mind, as loud as if someone had appeared next to him and spoken aloud.

Jon knew he hadn't made a decision regarding Grace. And that his indecision had hurt her, though he'd been trying not to do so. If he were being honest with himself—and there was no better time to be honest with himself—he'd known something was off since Halloween. Grace hadn't inconvenienced herself to see him. She didn't drive out to the ranch when she could've. She arrived late to church and claimed she was too tired to go to the picnic. Even when he invited her to dinner and kissed her good-night afterward, he didn't feel the same level of passion as he had previously.

"You messed up," he practically yelled at himself as

he entered the basement. He tore a bottle of water from the fridge and drained it, but it didn't cool the fire raging in his chest. With certain clarity, he knew only one thing would: Grace Lewis.

Even the thought of her name acted as a fire extinguisher, and the flames cooled. He still didn't know what to do short of calling a realtor and then a moving company to get everything he owned from Oklahoma City to Three Rivers.

He plucked his phone from his back pocket, but he didn't call a realtor. He called his brother instead. "Hey, Cam. What are you and Erika doing for Thanksgiving?" He listened while his brother talked about the celebration Erika's family had planned.

"Think they have room for one more?" Jon closed his eyes as he waited for his brother to answer. He wasn't ready to go crawling back to Grace, not yet. If he did that, he knew there'd be no turning back. And that decision required thoughtful prayer—and a talk with his brother, who had always been able to steer him in the right direction.

Chapter Seven

By the time the last pie got picked up on Wednesday evening, Grace never wanted to see another pecan again. Or another can of pumpkin. Or another dozen eggs. She collapsed in the armchair in her living room, her eyes drifting closed.

A sense of accomplishment flooded her. She'd done it. She'd organized, made, baked, and delivered ninety-five pies in one day.

"Just think what you could do with an industrial kitchen," she told herself as she went to put in a frozen pizza for dinner. Tomorrow, she'd drive out to the ranch for the first time in weeks, and the thought of seeing Jon drove her nerves into a frenzy. He hadn't tried to call her, not once. He hadn't texted. He hadn't liked anything of hers on Facebook.

She didn't know what his plans were now that he

wasn't going home to Oklahoma City, but she had to assume he would be at the homestead, ready to eat copious amounts of turkey and mashed potatoes.

Part of her mourned that he hadn't tried harder to get back together with her. The other part argued that Jonathan Carver was Jonathan Carver, and he hadn't tried to stay in touch when she'd moved eleven years ago. It wouldn't have been that hard. She could've done it too, but with him being silent, one year older, and about to graduate, she'd stayed away too.

She'd fantasized that this Christmas could've been celebrated as their eleven-year reunion, the opportunity they hadn't had as teenagers. Her heart hurt thinking about it, so she shelved the thoughts. She'd made it through the busiest day of her life, and tomorrow would be what tomorrow would be.

By the time she arrived at the ranch, lunch was about to start. She'd purposely left late, hoping to sneak in when the crowd wouldn't notice her. Of course, with Heidi there, that didn't work. She parted the sea of bodies and beelined for Grace as soon as she stepped through the French doors leading into the kitchen.

Heidi enveloped her in a motherly hug, and it was exactly what Grace needed in that moment. "Thank you, Heidi," she said as the woman stepped back.

"I was beginning to think you weren't going to come."

Grace swept the people in the kitchen, searching for Jon.

"He left last night," Heidi said. "Went to Wichita to be with his brother."

"Oh." Grace didn't know what else to say, didn't know how to make sense of the relief and simultaneous disappointment threading through her. She put on her happy face, the one she'd employed while she swept out her bakery for the last time, the one she wore while she drove from Dallas to Three Rivers, the one she used whenever she didn't want anyone to know how cracked under the surface she was.

Chelsea must've possessed some of her mother's x-ray vision, though, because after dinner and after pie and after the kids had been put down for naps and after the men had gone downstairs to watch football, she positioned herself next to Grace on the couch upstairs.

"Where's Jon?" she asked as she lifted a steaming cup of coffee to her lips.

"Wichita," Grace said.

"Heard you guys broke up."

Grace cut a sharp look in her direction. "From who?"

Chelsea waved her hand like the living room walls had told her. "He was in a real funk. It was obvious."

The idea of Jon being in a funk over their break-up brought Grace some satisfaction.

"What happened?" Chelsea asked as Kelly sat in the recliner opposite them.

Grace had always liked Chelsea, always trusted her with new recipes and old secrets. "He hates Three Rivers," she said.

Kelly gasped and Chelsea laughed. "I know how he feels."

"What?" Grace stared at her friend from Dallas.

"Remember when I moved here?" She glanced at Kelly. "I think I turned around three times on the way from Dallas. I hated it here...at first."

"I came back after a failed marriage," Kelly said. "Wasn't my idea of a great time either."

Grace had known Chelsea needed to leave Dallas. "I assumed you were...upset because of...you know."

"Danny's death," Chelsea said. "It's okay, Grace. I can talk about it now."

"I didn't know you didn't want to come to Three Rivers."

"Heavens, no." Chelsea laughed. "I left this place as fast as I could after high school. We both did."

Kelly nodded her agreement. "But I love it here now. It's quiet. Peaceful. Exactly where I want to raise my kids."

"All good points," Chelsea said, her eyebrows raised in Grace's direction.

"Jon and I—well, we didn't make it to the family and kids conversation. He wouldn't even talk about anything past Christmas." Bitterness surged up her throat.

Chelsea put her hand over Grace's. "Be patient with him. He probably doesn't know what he wants. Not everyone is as put together as you are."

Grace gave a mirthless laugh. "I am not put together." She felt like she was falling apart at the seams.

"You sure are," Chelsea said. "You went to pastry school, something you've dreamed about since you were ten. Who does that? Actually knows that they want to be when they're a child, and then does it?" She exchanged a glance with Kelly. "He's probably afraid. Worried he's not good enough for you."

"I bet he feels inadequate."

Grace listened to her friends in awe. She was not intimidating. No one—least of all Jon—should be afraid of her. And he was definitely good enough for her. The very idea that he wasn't seemed laughable. "Well, I think I'll go."

Chelsea squeezed her hand. "Okay, but Grace?" She peered up into Grace's face as she stood. "Just give him some time, all right?"

"Sure," Grace said, but she knew: Time didn't do

anything. She'd given her cupcakery months to succeed, and all she'd done was dig herself deeper into debt. She drove home, more determined than ever that she'd done the right thing when she'd cut Jon loose.

* * *

JON ARRIVED at the address his brother had given him. The two-story brick house seemed to loom over him, shout at him that he should be in Texas and not Oklahoma. But he hadn't been able to stay, to face Grace. And the thought of spending Thanksgiving alone appealed to him even less.

He'd done that before—spent Thanksgiving with hundreds of other men in Iraq. No family. Just the watered down version of turkey, and the hope that he'd be home in time for Cam's wedding at Easter.

He'd made it then. He could do this now. He got out of the car and walked up to the front door, which opened before he arrived. Cam, his older brother, beamed at him before clasping him in a tight hug. "It's been too long, Jon."

"You're the one who lives in Maryland." Jon chuckled, though he'd secretly resented Cam for years because he'd left the carpentry business for Jon to handle. Now, though, none of those old feelings surfaced, and Jon realized he'd forgiven Cam, moved on.

Cam released him and welcomed him into the house. His wife, Erika, stood in the living room. A petite brunette, Jon felt like he might break her when he hugged her hello. She introduced him to her parents, who Jon thanked over and over for adding him to their guest list so last minute.

"What happened in Texas, anyway?" Cam asked.

Jon flashed him a warning look and smiled. The gesture felt wrong on his face. "I was plannin' to spend Thanksgiving in Oklahoma City," he said. "But *someone* gave *someone else* plane tickets to New York."

That shut Cam up. Thankfully. Jon wanted to talk about Grace, but in private, without the presence of several strangers, no matter how accommodating they were. That moment didn't come until much later that evening, after visiting and dinner and coffee on the screened-in back porch. A humming space heater kept the airy room warm enough, and the hot liquid definitely helped.

Erika swept a kiss across Cam's mouth and headed into the house with her parents and brother, leaving Jon alone with Cam. He enjoyed the silence for a few minutes, searching for a way to bring up Grace without giving too much away.

In the end, he simply blurted, "So I met a woman in Texas."

Cam put his coffee mug down and faced Jon. "Oh, yeah?"

"You might remember her." Though Jon didn't really think so. Cam was three years older than Jon, and Jon a year older than Grace. "Yeah, Grace Lewis."

Cam's blank expression indicated he did not remember Grace. And why should he? He hadn't been the one entranced by the woman's navy blue eyes, or captured by her laugh, or intrigued by her obsession with baking.

So Jon reminded him, though Cam still didn't have any memories of Jon's high school homecoming dance or Grace's sudden removal from his life. "And now she's back." He ran his hands through his hair. He'd left his cowboy hat in Texas, and he suddenly felt naked without it. "What are the chances she'd be in Three Rivers when I am?"

"Probably less than one percent." Cam gazed into the distance, though his degree was in statistics, and surely he knew the exact odds of Grace and Jon being in the same small Texas town at the same time.

Jon stewed, wishing he knew how to articulate to his brother what his problem was, what help he needed. Instead, he told him about Grace, about his hesitation to stay in tiny Three Rivers. He finally fell silent after he said, "Tell me what to do."

"Nope." Cam exhaled and stretched his arms above his head. "Not gonna tell you what to do, Jonny. You always wanted me to choose for you, and I did when we were growing up. But I can't do that here."

"Then what would you do?"

Cam leveled his gaze at Jon. "I'd ask myself if I liked this woman enough to want to see if I could fall in love with her. And if I do like her that much, I'd figure out what to do to keep her in my life long enough to know if we could have a future together."

Jon started nodding halfway through Cam's statement. "I like her enough."

"Do you hate Three Rivers that much?"

"I—" Jon's throat narrowed, and familiar frustration ran through him. "I don't know."

"I think you know what to do, then." Cam stood and entered the house, the screen door slapping behind him as he left Jon alone on the screened-in porch. He stared at the unfamiliar horizon and wondered why he cared where he lived. If Grace was there, he'd be happy. And if she wasn't....

He reached for his phone and dialed her, hoping she'd be forgiving enough to answer. Her line rang and rang, wringing his stomach tighter and tighter. She didn't pick up, and something clogged the back of Jon's throat.

Could he jump in his truck and drive the six hours back to Three Rivers? Show up on her doorstep and beg her to take him back?

He dialed her again, and this time he left a message. "Hey, Grace. It's Jon. I've been...." He sighed and threw caution to the wind. "I've been so stupid. Please forgive me. And please call me back." He wanted to add something more, but he couldn't say, "I love you." So he hung up with extreme exasperation pressing against the back of his tongue.

A half hour passed, wherein Jon pressed the power button on his phone every thirty seconds just to make sure it still had a charge. Finally, it rang. He fumbled it in his haste to answer, especially when Grace's name came up on the screen.

"Grace," he said. "Hey."

"Happy Thanksgiving," she said.

Jon tried to gauge her mood by her voice, but his heart beat so loudly in his ears, he couldn't. "Happy Thanksgiving to you too. Did you get my message?"

"Yes." A door slammed on her end of the line. "I didn't have service on the way back from the ranch. And you're lucky it's Thanksgiving and I'm feeling extra grateful for all I have—which I'll admit, I hope that includes you."

The wave of relief cascading over Jon rivaled a tsunami. He collapsed back to the chair, not quite sure when he'd stood. "I'm so sorry, Grace. I wish I was there to tell you in person."

"Hearing it in your voice is enough."

"So what now?"

"Well, Jon, we'll need to talk about important things when you get back."

He leaned back in his chair, unwilling to let her go now that he had her on the line. "What about tonight?"

"I'm too tired to talk about serious things tonight." She yawned. "I was up early to make the pies for Thanksgiving dinner. Tell me about your trip."

Jon imagined Grace reclined in the armchair in her living room, her eyes already closed. He smiled and began to talk.

Chapter Eight

Grace's skin itched with anticipation. With the need to be doing something. She wasn't good at sitting, never had been. But with all the holiday orders fulfilled and nothing to do until Monday—and she wasn't even sure what she'd do then—Grace had a few days to herself.

Problem was, she didn't know what to *do* with herself. She'd driven through her favorite java hut and watched the sun rise over the river on the south side of town. Jon was driving back from Wichita today, but it was a long way, and she wasn't expecting him until at least afternoon.

Black Friday in Three Rivers started later than in other areas—no lines around the block before five a.m. here—and gradually the town came to life. Grace walked down Main Street, ducking into a few shops until she finally found a beautiful clothing boutique. She browsed through the clothes, the scarves, the shoes, looking for something cute to wear to church.

She tried on several things, made her purchases from a kind dark-haired woman named Andy, and headed home. It was only nine o'clock.

A level of exhaustion Grace hadn't experienced since pastry school engulfed her, and she dropped her shopping bags at the mouth of the hall and dropped to the couch.

She woke to the gentle pressure of Jon's lips against her forehead, the masculine smell of pine trees and wood smoke making her smile and open her eyes.

"Hey," he whispered. "Sorry to wake you. You just looked too beautiful not to kiss."

"Smooth," she said as she lifted her arms to hug him. "I'm glad you came back." She enjoyed the weight of him against her, the electricity zipping down her neck when he kissed her there, the absolute joy coursing through her that he'd called, apologized, come back.

"Are you too tired to talk?" He traced his lips up her throat, and all thoughts of talking fled her mind. By the time he finally kissed her mouth, Grace's muscles felt like warm marshmallows. She twined her fingers through his dark, silky hair, and gave her whole self to him.

She finally put a knuckle of space between them, and his labored breathing indicated he enjoyed kissing her as much as she enjoyed kissing him. But there had to be more to this relationship than hot sparks and great kissing.

"What time is it?" she asked.

"Nearly two." He sat back on his haunches as she came to a sitting position on the couch. "Want to go grab lunch?"

Her stomach answered with a roar. She raked her fingers through her hair, trying to deny she'd slept for five hours and failing. She'd definitely slept for five hours. Jon stood and slid his hand down her shoulder. "You ready?"

"Sure." She collected her purse and followed him out to his truck. Her stomach twisted and untwisted on the drive there. She wanted him to start the conversation, because she felt like she'd said everything she needed to already.

But he told her about his visit with his brother, and the drive from Wichita, and how he wished he'd been able to taste one of her pies. After being shown to a booth, Jon finally fell silent. Grace ordered sweet tea and fixed her gaze on him, almost like she could communicate telepathically with him.

The waitress left to get their drinks, and Jon squirmed. "I'm not great at making decisions."

Grace blinked, unsure of where he was going. "Okay."

"No, it's not okay." He rubbed his hand up the back of his neck and looked away. "It's why I'm still in construction. I couldn't decide if I should go to school and if I did, what I should do."

"You don't like carpentry?"

"No, I do." He let out a frustrated breath. "I don't know how to articulate what I'm feeling." The waitress returned and took their orders, and Jon gulped his soda before meeting her eye again.

"You've always known what you wanted to be. And you went out there and did it." He reached across the table and took her hands in his. "I love that about you. But I'm not like that. I was raised in construction and I liked it. Cam didn't want to stick around, and I didn't have anything else to do...." He shrugged. "It's not that I'm *un*happy. It's just that I didn't *choose* carpentry. I'm not good at making choices. It's like...it's like, if I do, then I might not get what I want. I might be disappointed. I might fail."

Grace's chest heaved with emotion. Here was this handsome, talented man, looking at her with all the vulnerability of a scared boy. She squeezed his hands and opened her eyes wide to try to keep the tears back.

She couldn't quite get herself to speak yet, choked

up as she was. He blinked a couple of times, the tendons in his neck tight, tight, tight.

"Do you know why I moved to Three Rivers?" Grace fought against the fear of telling him about all her failures. But at least she had them. Maybe if he knew about them, he'd know life could be great, despite setbacks and disappointments.

"To help Heidi open her bakery."

Grace shook her head. "Yes, because I needed a job after my cupcake shop in Dallas failed." She inhaled, relieved the previous emotion had settled back into her stomach. "And that was after it took me three tries to get into culinary school."

"Grace," Jon said, and she loved hearing him say her name. "I didn't know. I'm sorry." His jaw tightened and he let out an angry hiss. "Here I am crying about failing, and you.... I'm sorry."

She shook her head. "No, don't feel bad. I was just trying to let you know that I've failed. I understand the fear of it. But at least—" She cut herself off before she could say something that would hurt him further, drive him farther from her.

"At least you've tried," he finished for her. His fury faded, leaving behind the scared man again. "I want to try, Grace. With you. Can you give me a few more weeks to try?"

"Of course."

"You didn't even think about it."

"I don't need to think about it." And she didn't. She liked Jon, always had. She wanted to see if they could have a future together as badly as she'd wanted culinary school, as much as she'd wanted her cupcakery in Dallas, as desperately as she'd tried to hold onto it before admitting defeat.

Maybe she was doing the same thing here. She wasn't sure. She just knew she liked him enough to think she might be able to love him, and she didn't want to walk away before either of them knew for sure.

"You're too forgiving," he said.

"That's impossible," she said. "I don't think anyone can actually be *too* forgiving. Can they?"

"In some situations, yes, I think someone can be too forgiving."

"Well, this isn't one of those situations." She pulled her hands back across the table as the waitress appeared with their food. "I want to try too, Jon."

He flashed her a grateful smile, and Grace enjoyed a meal for the first time since she'd told Jon they should be done.

* * *

A week later, Jon had experienced more happiness and more heartache than he ever had in his life. He'd realized that he'd never really lived before. Because he'd never *chosen* his life. As he realized his shortcomings, he struggled, but as he made decisions, the joy superseded the tough times.

How's your day going? he texted to Grace during his lunch hour.

Okay, she said. *I went for doughnuts this morning, and they didn't have any bacon maple bars.*

Jon wanted to make Grace happy, give her everything she desired. *Sorry, babe,* he texted. Then he called the bakery and asked them about a special order. They agreed to make a bacon maple bar the following day and save it for Grace. They didn't deliver, but Jon would drive to town himself and take the doughnut to her.

When he knocked on her front door, she didn't answer right away. He knew she was awake—the woman rose in the middle of the night. Concern spiked within him when she still didn't come after he'd knocked again.

He didn't want to call her—wanted the doughnut to be a surprise—but he pulled out his phone and paced down her front sidewalk. His thumb hovered above the call button when she came jogging down the road toward him.

She saw him a nanosecond after he noticed her,

and he shoved his phone in his back pocket. She pulled out her earbuds. "What are you doing here?"

"You run?"

"I have to do something to keep the sweets I eat in check." She eyed the white bag in his hand. "What is that?"

"Bacon maple bar." He grinned as he held the pastry toward her.

"You didn't." She took the bag and peered inside. When she lifted her eyes back to his, Jon saw admiration in them. "Thank you." She stepped into his arms and kissed him. He didn't care that she was sweaty; he kissed her back.

Chapter Nine

Over the next two weeks, Grace became used to waking up to late-night texts from Jon. He spoiled her constantly, asking her what her interests were, and planning romantic dates to the lesser known attractions in Three Rivers. Once, he'd taken her on an alphabet date—two of them, actually—where they did everything from apple eating contests for the letter A to taste all the types of cheeses at the cheese factory for T. She'd ridden horses, hiked hills, visited the botanical gardens.

Three Rivers had become ingrained in her soul. She loved the shops along Main Street. The friendliness of the townspeople. The close-knit community.

With the bakery only two weeks from opening, she'd started spending her days in the retail space downtown. Heidi had bought the end corner of a building that had suffered fire damage. She'd spent a lot to restore it, and the kitchen gleamed in the early morning light bulbs. Grace arrived at three-thirty and made muffins, brownies, and cookies before Heidi showed up at five to begin the bread.

By six-thirty, when they planned to open, Grace had a tray of samples ready for anyone who wanted to drive or walk by. With the amount of people tasting their toasted sourdough with apricot jam, or the lemon poppyseed muffins, Grace felt sure the bakery would be a success.

She left the bakery just after noon and strolled down the street, her thoughts circling a gift for Jon. With Christmas only days away, she needed something, and fast. She'd gotten to know him better these past few weeks, when they were finally able to talk about real things, their likes and dislikes, their dreams, their worries.

She'd learned that he did love construction, but didn't like being tied down. The freedom for him to travel to job sites was important to him. She'd learned that he loved staying up late, and Neapolitan ice cream, and watching documentaries. She'd already known he was a hard worker, but the fact was driven home as he and Brett labored to finish what she'd learned was a new horse training facility before Christmas.

"One more day," he'd told her yesterday, which meant he'd be done today.

He was planning to stay in Three Rivers for Christmas and the New Year as well as be there to support her and Heidi as the bakery opened on January fourth. After that...he'd promised he'd know by Christmas Eve, only three short days away.

She'd known he loved his family, but she'd learned he also wanted one of his own. She'd known he was smart, but she'd figured out that his preferred wardrobe colors consisted of shades of blue, brown, and black.

She'd already purchased a new shirt for him—in red—and a five-gallon container of Neapolitan ice cream. But she wanted more for him. But what, she couldn't quite put her finger on. She'd already wandered the aisles of the supermarket, the hardware store, and the western wear shop. No luck. Nothing that stood out and screamed *Jon!*

He was planning a private Christmas Eve dinner for them at her house. She'd promised him a dessert he wouldn't forget—she had orange chocolate coffee cake and a coconut panna cotta on the menu. The ingredients had been bought. She'd mailed her parents a present a week ago. A lanyard specially made with the bakery logo Chelsea had designed sat wrapped under her mini tree for Heidi.

Grace ducked into a jewelry store, but immediately

regretted the decision. All the diamonds made her think of marriage, and she didn't even know if Jon would still be in town two weeks from now.

Maybe it didn't hurt to look.... Grace examined the cases of rings, finding green and blue gemstones among the purple and white.

"Looking for yourself?" an elderly woman asked.

"No." Grace smiled. "Just browsing." And daydreaming. The woman left her to look while she helped another couple. Grace paused in front of the engagement rings, thinking through what she might like. She'd dated a few men in New York, but chefs often thought highly of themselves and nothing had stuck for longer than a few months. Certainly no one had prompted her to think in diamonds.

She stilled, her heart racing as though she'd just sprinted the last hundred yards of a run. Jon Carver was diamond-worthy. She'd wear his ring with pride. She'd marry him and be happy.

Because she loved him.

A smile moved across her face, stretched down into her soul. She hadn't prayed to know if Jon was the right man for her. Somehow, since she was a junior in high school, she'd known. Now, she prayed that she could be the right woman for him—and that he would know it before it came time for him to leave town.

* * *

Jon almost went off the road three times on the way to Grace's. The Christmas Eve wind had brought in a storm, but that wasn't the real reason he couldn't keep his truck aimed in a straight line.

No, that blame fell on the little, black, jewelry box sitting on the seat next to him. He'd never been so nervous to give a gift in his life. Never been so nervous to eat a meal.

It's Grace, he told himself, and the nerves faded for a few minutes. But inevitably, they came roaring back. The ingredients for their candlelit dinner sat next to him, and she'd promised she wouldn't bother him while he mashed and basted and sautéed.

She welcomed him with a quick side hug before she took a few of the grocery bags he carried. "It smells fantastic in here," he said, sniffing to identify the scent. "What is that?"

"It's a surprise," she singsonged. "You'll have to be patient." She toted her bags into the kitchen, but Jon paused by the tiny pine tree she'd set up on her end table. Acting quickly, he slipped the jewelry box out of the grocery sack and under the tree. Several other gifts sat there, and he felt certain she wouldn't notice.

He joined her in the kitchen and started unpacking potatoes and green beans and onions.

"Mm," she said. "A man after my own heart."

He laughed as she petted a potato. "You have the oven ready?"

"As instructed."

He nodded toward the front door. "I left the ham in my truck. It's already done. Just needs to be warmed."

"Be right back."

Jon couldn't help watching her walk away, and the feeling he'd been searching for these past few weeks manifested itself—again.

He was in love with Grace Lewis. He smiled at the repeated realization, his heart doing the tango as he thought about moving to Three Rivers.

You have to do it, he told himself. *She's worth it.*

She came back through the front door, laden with the heavy baking dish. She slid the ham into the oven and he slid his hands around her waist. "Grace, I have to tell you something."

She seemed to melt into him, seemed made to fit against him.

For one moment, his brain rebelled. Wouldn't control his vocal cords long enough to get them to produce sound. He swallowed and found his center when she reached up and ran her fingers through his hair.

He gazed into her eyes and saw a life worth having. A life worth having only if it was with her.

"I love you, Grace."

She sucked in a surprised breath and blinked.

"I'm going to move to Three Rivers so we can be together." He hadn't intended to give her his gift before dinner. But he found his feet moving toward the living room, and his hand gently guiding a silent Grace with him.

"I don't know exactly how you feel, because you haven't said anything. I know you've been giving me time and whatever, and I appreciate that. But I've made my decision." He reached for the box and picked it up. "I prayed about it, and the answer was clear. So though I might not like Three Rivers, I love you. And because your life is here, I want to be here."

He dropped to one knee and Grace pressed both hands to her mouth, her eyes shining with what Jon hoped were joyful tears.

"It might be fast, and I haven't asked you when you envisioned your wedding, but Grace, will you marry me?" He flipped open the box the way he'd been practicing for a solid week and held the ring up for her inspection.

She didn't even look at it. She couldn't seem to look away from him, and he gazed steadily back, hoping to be the anchor she relied on in her life.

Worry had just wormed its way under his skin when she nodded, a tear fell, and she said, "Yes," between her fingers.

In a fluid motion, he stood and wrapped her in an embrace. When she stretched up to kiss him, Jon felt sure he was the luckiest man in all of Texas.

"Best Christmas gift ever," she whispered, her lips practically touching his. "I love you too, Jon."

He'd thought "yes" was the best thing he'd ever heard, but hearing Grace tell him she loved him sounded a hundred times sweeter. He grinned as he slid the ring on her finger and kissed her again.

"Well, what'd you get me?"

She giggled but didn't move out of the circle of his arms. "I didn't put it under the tree. It's in my bedroom."

"You gonna make me wait?" He touched his lips to his favorite spot below her ear.

She sighed against him. "I guess not." She stepped away and hurried down the hall. She returned a moment later with a hatbox. "You see now why I didn't put it under the tree." She handed him the gift.

He opened it, expecting to see a cowboy hat—and he did. One of the finest cowboy hats someone could buy. "Grace." He glanced up at her. "This is too much."

She folded her arms. "You bought me a diamond. Go on. Put it on."

He took out the slate gray hat, the weight and texture of it perfect. He placed the hat on his head, and genuine happiness poured through him.

"I noticed you favor blues and grays," she said. "I thought this would match most of what you wear."

He locked eyes with her. "You notice what I wear?"

She flashed him a coy smile. "You are a big, strong, handsome man."

He growled, pulled her toward him, and kissed the best Christmas present he'd ever received.

The End

Read on for a sneak peek at the next book in the Three Rivers Ranch Romance™ series - **THE TWELFTH TOWN!**

Sneak Peek! The Twelfth Town
Chapter One

The long row of cabins at Three Rivers Ranch had never looked more glorious than they did to Taryn Tucker. She stood at the end of them on a Monday morning, her gaze stretching across all twelve of them, the same way she had last week after she'd been offered the job of cleaning them.

Playing maid was a long way from having a professional makeup artist paint her face and a stylist make sure every strand of hair fell the right way. But Taryn much preferred this life to the one she used to have.

Or at least she hoped she would. With eleven small towns behind her, she desperately wanted to find one to live in for a while. She tucked her newly dyed black hair into a ponytail and then stuffed the ends into a messy bun before stooping for her cleaning supplies. Might as well get started.

She thought about the apartment she'd been able to find in Three Rivers, a town she'd stumbled upon quite by accident the week before. She'd never seen quite such an enthusiastic Halloween celebration before. Not even in New Orleans, where she'd been assigned one October a few years ago—and they knew how to celebrate death in Louisiana.

She'd used the last of her meager paycheck from town number eleven, where she'd worked bagging groceries until she got too nervous to stay, to pay for a hotel for a couple of nights until she found the one-bedroom unit above the barber shop on Main Street.

They won't follow you this far, Taryn told herself as she mounted the steps to the first cabin, the one closest to the homestead where she'd been instructed to replenish her cleaning supplies.

At least Taryn hoped they wouldn't. She wasn't even sure who "they" were, only that someone from her former employer wanted to know where she'd disappeared to. As if the public humiliation she'd caused as well as endured couldn't be viewed twenty-four hours a day via the Internet.

Six months had passed. Surely the news station would find another story to focus on, especially in a city the size of Corpus Christi. Taryn had been praying for a hurricane, and though they sat in the thick of the season, God had not granted her requests for such a storm. It was just as well. She didn't want to be responsible for tragedy and death just to get the attention off her messed up personal life.

She mourned the loss of such a life as she fitted the master key into the lock. Still, the owner of the ranch, Squire Ackerman, hadn't seemed to recognize her— *and why would he?* she asked herself.

Corpus Christi television stations didn't broadcast to dinky Three Rivers. But somehow, Taryn carried the weight of who she'd been and it cumbered her shoulders, weighed her down.

She entered the cabin and set her bucket of supplies on the floor so she could return to retrieve the vacuum cleaner. Apparently cleaning the cowboy cabins was a brand-new job; Squire had never hired someone to do it before. According to him, his cowboys right now were of the messy variety.

Taryn lugged the vacuum up the steps and into the cabin, pausing to wipe the first inklings of sweat from her forehead. She clutched the bucket with one hand and towed the vacuum behind her with the other as she headed for the bedroom in the back of the quiet cabin. She'd mapped out a plan of attack to get three of the twelve cabins done each day, and that started with working from the back to the front. Each cabin would be done in two hours, with fifteen-minute breaks in between.

Squire had agreed to her plan during the second interview, and given her the requested four-day work week. Taryn was really looking forward to a three-day weekend each week, and her spirits lifted as she barged through the bedroom door.

"Hey!" A man stood there, barely wearing a pair of jeans. He fumbled with the zipper while Taryn stared. With his pants securely in place, he folded his arms across his bare chest. His impressively wide bare chest.

"Who might you be?" He grinned at her, an action which made her mortification fall down a notch. He reached for a white undershirt lying on the unmade bed and pulled it over his sandy-haired head. He obviously hadn't shaved that morning—or any morning in the past month. Red and lighter brown salted his beard, which he'd trimmed neatly along his jawline.

Taryn swallowed, unable to find her voice. His blue-gray eyes sucked at her. They seemed filled with lightning, with laughter, with life. She envied him immediately.

"It's no big deal," he said. "I just don't normally have pretty women back here." He pulled a blue and black plaid shirt from his closet and put it on. "My name's Kenny Stockton." He stepped toward her and offered his hand.

She dropped her cleaning bucket and put her hand inside his, and it looked child-sized comparatively. She swallowed and took a calming breath. He didn't seem upset she'd walked in on him. "Taryn Tucker." She cringed at her near-perfect delivery, as if she was signing off one of her newscasts. *I'm Taryn Tucker. Good-night, Corpus Christi.*

"Pleased to meet you, Taryn Tucker." He looked at her curiously, but he didn't seem to recognize her. She glanced around for a television in his bedroom and didn't find one. Her muscles softened, and she allowed herself to smile at the handsome cowboy who still held her hand.

"Sorry I barged on in," she said. "I didn't think anyone would be home. Squire said the cowhands are up early to do their jobs."

Kenny slid his hand away from hers. "Yeah, I got real dirty during the haul this mornin'. Came back to shower before heading over to the admin trailer for my next assignment." He glanced around, as if just now noticing that beds could be made. "Sorry about the mess."

She forced herself to give a light giggle. "That's my job. If you go doin' it, I won't get paid." And she needed the money. Her salary had long dried up, and the hourly-wage jobs she'd been getting by with never seemed to pay enough.

At least you're not sleeping in your car, she thought as she searched for an outlet to plug in the vacuum.

That night—though it had only been a single night—had been one of the worst of her life. Worse than the night she'd said no to her boyfriend's proposal on live TV.

A chill ran down her back, and she lifted her hand in acknowledgement when Kenny said he was heading out. Relief spread through her when the front door banged closed behind him, and Taryn sank onto his bed. No tears came—she'd cried them all out in the first three months.

Just pure exhaustion. She needed to get out of Texas if she had any hope of living a normal life. But as it always did, the thought of returning home to South Dakota brought on a wave of nausea Taryn had learned to swallow down and breathe through. Her parents hadn't seen the debacle—she doubted they had any idea that she'd left Corpus Christi six months ago—but she didn't want to return to Bottle Hollow and explain why. After all, she'd vowed never to return when she'd left a decade ago.

She spoke to her mother from time to time, but her father still hadn't opened the lines of communication. Some words took longer to fade to whispers, Taryn supposed. Or perhaps her father was as stubborn as her mother always said he was.

She inhaled deeply to inflate her chest and focused on the closet in front of her. A gray camouflage hint of fabric caught her eye, and she sprang to her feet and shoved the clothes which concealed the uniform to the left.

U.S. Marines.

Her chest rose and fell in shallow breaths. *Stockton* sat above the right breast pocket, and Taryn wondered where he'd been stationed, how he'd gotten out of the Marines, and why he'd chosen ranching instead of something like law enforcement the way her brother had.

She took a deep drag of air, expecting to find the woodsy, spicy scent of Collin. She didn't. She hadn't since his death three years ago. Still, something about this desert cammie called to her.

Another breath revealed a new scent, one that wrapped through her soul and wound around her toes. This one smelled like fresh cotton, and outdoorsy dryer sheets, and something deeply masculine.

Kenny's scent.

Taryn closed her eyes and reveled in it, a fistful of his uniform clutched in her fingers. Something beyond the house snapped, and her eyes snapped open. She stumbled away from his personal belongings. Embarrassment flooded her.

"Get a grip," she muttered to herself as she started the vacuum. She attacked the clutter and dust in Kenny's cabin with vigor. After all, she wasn't in town to get involved with another marine, even if he smelled as wonderful as she imagined heaven to be. Even if his eyes carried a twinkle and his deep voice sang to her soul and his muscles testified of his impressive physique.

No, she'd had enough of cops and servicemen. Enough of watching them die, the way her brother had. Enough of dating them and then humiliating them when they proposed to her.

Familiar remorse combined with an inexplicable rage hit her right behind the breastbone. Chris should've known not to surprise her like that. Nothing about their year-long relationship had suggested she'd enjoy an on-air proposal.

Her refusal *was* his fault, and yet she'd lost everything because of it. Taryn left Kenny's cabin in tip-top shape, determined not to let her ex-boyfriend into her thoughts, her decision-making, her life. Not anymore.

As she entered the next cabin, she looked up into the rafters of the porch as if gazing toward heaven. *Help me find what I need here,* she prayed. If only she knew what that was and how to get it.

"What's your deal today?"

Kenny looked up at Lawrence's question, his mind

still trying to focus on organizing the words into a sentence that made sense. He blinked and looked at the horse he'd been brushing. "No deal."

"I've been talking to you, and you don't respond." Lawrence led his horse into the stall and latched it. "It's like you've got a lot on your mind." He leaned against the fence and grinned. "But you're Kenny, so that can't be true."

Kenny chuckled with his friend. "I suppose I've been distracted today." Distracted by a gorgeous pair of brown eyes and hair he'd been speculating on its true color for most of the day. The black on Taryn obviously came from a bottle.

"You been lookin' at a new horse?"

A twinge of disdain pinched behind Kenny's eyes. But Lawrence wouldn't automatically assume Kenny had been distracted by a woman. He rarely made it past the third date, and the last woman he'd been out with declined his dinner invitation, claiming he was "too happy."

Well, Kenny didn't know how to be unhappy. Didn't really seem to be in his nature, and he certainly wasn't going to apologize about his glass-half-full attitude. His time in the Marines had taught him to see the darkness, the evil, the horrors of this world. He didn't want to exist there all the time.

He thanked God everyday that he'd been able to

serve his country without losing his life. So many others didn't. He'd served two four-year terms of active service before leaving the Marines, before wandering the country in search of what to do next, before he'd found Three Rivers Ranch. His father had known Garth Ahlstrom in Montana, and Kenny had come to Texas a few years ago looking for a job. Garth hired him the same day. Another blessing.

"Hello?" Lawrence waved his hand in front of Kenny's eyes. "Must be a beautiful horse."

"Hm." Kenny didn't correct him. So he'd thought Taryn was pretty. Every man who looked at her surely thought that too. She was petite and polite, which led Kenny to believe she'd been raised in the South.

The heat from her hand still burned in his, and he fisted his fingers as he finished his last chore before heading back to his cabin. For one small moment, he fantasized about walking in on Taryn. But the idea was ridiculous. Squire had hired her to clean all the cabins, as well as the administration building. It wouldn't take her all day to clean his cabin, though it was a bit of a pig sty.

Sure enough, when he tried to enter his cabin, the door was locked. He fished his keys from his pocket and entered the quiet cabin. His roommate, Charlie, would be home in a few minutes, and Kenny took the opportunity while he was alone to admire the freshly vacuumed rugs, the straight pillows on the couch, and his crisply made bed.

Kenny wondered where Taryn had come from. He hadn't seen her at church previously, but that was his only interaction with anyone off the ranch. Maybe she didn't go to church. And it wasn't like he went every single week either.

"Wow, this place looks great." Charlie entered the cabin and kicked his dirty boots onto the clean rug. "What're you thinkin' for dinner?"

Kenny hadn't thought of anything but Taryn for hours. He hadn't discovered how to get her number, or what her schedule at the ranch would be, or anything. He didn't want to ask. Didn't want anyone to know of his interest.

The wind shook the windows as Kenny said, "Pizza or spaghetti."

"You cooking?"

"Sure." He stepped into the kitchen and pulled out a stock pot.

"This place smells like lilacs," Charlie commented, and Kenny smiled as he salted the pasta water.

* * *

THE NEXT MORNING, Kenny didn't see Taryn on his way to the administration building. Garth had messaged all the cowhands about a mandatory meeting that morning, instead of just heading out to their usual chores.

"Maybe we'll get our new assignments," Charlie commented.

"Nah." Kenny grinned at him as they climbed the steps to the building. "We just got new ones last month."

"Yeah, you're right." Charlie lowered his head against the wind, his tone resigned. Kenny didn't much care what his chore was, though there were definitely less desirable jobs around the ranch. Kenny was just glad to be out of a uniform, working the hours of the day away, and living a carefree life.

A flash of black hair caught his attention, but he didn't truly have a chance to see if it was Taryn or not before Charlie opened the door and ushered Kenny into the admin building. They took seats and waited for Garth to appear. By the time he finally did, Kenny had listened to Lawrence and Charlie bicker good-naturedly about whose dog was smarter and why.

"Storm comin' in," Garth said as a way to call the cowboys to order. It worked. "I reckon we have today to get the animals secure, get the barns all closed up, and the rest of the week, we'll be working on indoor improvements."

Some of the cowboys shuffled their feet, but not

Kenny. He didn't mind working inside any more than he did outside. Someone asked what kind of indoor improvements, and Garth mentioned painting and appliance repair in some of the cabins, maybe laying new flooring in a couple of them, and other home improvement items Kenny had never done. But he could wipe a brush up and down and follow written directions.

The meeting ended with assignments to get the livestock on the ranch secured, and Kenny got assigned along with a half-dozen cowhands to ride out and check on the herd. They'd hunker down next to the tree line for some security, and Kenny labored with the other men to make the field smaller. Keeping the cattle in a group would help them stay calm, and it was only supposed to rain. Buckets, but just rain.

Kenny drove another nail into the plywood back Garth had instructed they build on the existing roof structure that protected the feeding troughs. The cattle wouldn't be able to access the hay from both sides, but the chances of their feed lasting through the storm increased with the additional wall.

"Roof's secure," Lawrence said from the other side of the structure. "This is almost done."

"Great work," Garth said. "The hay'll be here in a few minutes. We'll get that out, and we'll head home."

Kenny nailed faster, swinging the hammer with

near lightning speed. He'd had enough of the wind pulling at his hat and whipping through his ears. He wasn't sure Texas ever got truly cold, but with this wind and the threatening gray sky, a chill skated over his arms.

The trucks arrived and the men set to work filling the troughs. Grass still grew in this field too, but no one would be out to check the herd for three days, and Garth wasn't the kind of foreman who took chances. Kenny knew he'd come out in a hailstorm to check on the cattle if he was concerned about them.

He finished up his job and helped get the last of the hay out. With fresh water in the lower trough, Garth called, "Let's get outta here, boys!" He flattened his hand against his head as the wind kicked up, and Kenny started toward his horse. He led two along behind him as a couple of the boys got a ride in the back of the truck.

"You okay there, Kenny?" Garth asked as he leaned out the window of the truck.

"Just fine, boss."

"It's just you and Aaron. Keep an eye on each other."

"Sure thing, boss." But Kenny didn't look up. The weather threw dust and dirt and debris into his face, and he used his cowboy hat to keep himself protected. At one point, he spotted Aaron ahead of him on the horizon, also leading two horses. Kenny whistled a tune he'd learned in the Marines as Orion, his faithful black-and-white horse, plodded on home.

He'd just passed the cabin in section twelve when something floated to him on the wind. He jerked his head up, searching for the source of the cry. Maybe it was an animal—the prairie played home to more than just cattle, he knew.

His pulse pounding and his blood beating through his veins, he scanned the horizon. Nothing.

The cry came again, a high-pitched noise without shape or meaning. He whipped his head left, and there, so far out where the land met the angry sky, he spotted a dark figure.

A human figure.

* * *

Read THE TWELFTH TOWN today! Look for it by scanning the QR code below.

Second Chance Ranch: A Three Rivers Ranch Romance™ (Book 1): After his deployment, injured and discharged Major Squire Ackerman returns to Three Rivers Ranch, wanting to forgive Kelly for ignoring him a decade ago. He'd like to provide the stable life she needs, but with old wounds opening and a ranch on the brink of financial collapse, it will take patience and faith to make their second chance possible.

Third Time's the Charm: A Three Rivers Ranch Romance™ (Book 2): First Lieutenant Peter Marshall has a truck-load of debt and no way to provide for a family, but Chelsea helps him see past all the obstacles, all the scars. With so many unknowns, can Pete and Chelsea develop the love, acceptance, and faith needed to find their happily ever after?

Fourth and Long: A Three Rivers Ranch Romance™ (Book 3): Commander Brett Murphy goes to Three Rivers Ranch to find some rest and relaxation with his Army buddies. Having his ex-wife show up with a seven-year-old she claims is his son is anything but the R&R he craves. Kate needs to make amends, and Brett needs to find forgiveness, but are they too late to find their happily ever after?

Fifth Generation Cowboy: A Three Rivers Ranch Romance™ (Book 4): Tom Lovell has watched his friends find their true happiness on Three Rivers Ranch, but everywhere he looks, he only sees friends. Rose Reyes has been bringing her daughter out to the ranch for equine therapy for months, but it doesn't seem to be working. Her challenges with Mari are just as frustrating as ever. Could Tom be exactly what Rose needs? Can he remove his friendship blinders and find love with someone who's been right in front of him all this time?

Sixth Street Love Affair: A Three Rivers Ranch Romance™ (Book 5): After losing his wife a few years back, Garth Ahlstrom thinks he's ready for a second chance at love. But Juliette Thompson has a secret that could destroy their budding relationship. Can they find the strength, patience, and faith to make things work?

The Seventh Sergeant: A Three Rivers Ranch Romance™ (Book 6): Life has finally started to settle down for Sergeant Reese Sanders after his devastating injury overseas. Discharged from the Army and now with a good job at Courage Reins, he's finally found happiness—until a horrific fall puts him right back where he was years ago: Injured and depressed. Carly Watters, Reese's new veteran care coordinator, dislikes small towns almost as much as she loathes cowboys. But she finds herself faced with both when she gets assigned to Reese's case. Do they have the humility and faith to make their relationship more than professional?

Eight Second Ride: A Three Rivers Ranch Romance™ (Book 7): Ethan Greene loves his work at Three Rivers Ranch, but he can't seem to find the right woman to settle down with. When sassy yet vulnerable Brynn Bowman shows up at the ranch to recruit him back to the rodeo circuit, he takes a different approach with the barrel racing champion. His patience and newfound faith pay off when a friendship--and more--starts with Brynn. But she wants out of the rodeo circuit right when Ethan wants to rejoin. Can they find the path God wants them to take and still stay together?

The Ninth Inning: A Three Rivers Ranch Romance™ (Book 8): The Christmas season has never felt like such a burden to boutique owner Andrea Larsen. But with Mama gone and the holidays upon her, Andy finds herself wishing she hadn't been so quick to judge her former boyfriend, cowboy Lawrence Collins. Well, Lawrence hasn't forgotten about Andy either, and he devises a plan to get her out to the ranch so they can reconnect. Do they have the faith and humility to patch things up and start a new relationship?

Ten Days in Town: A Three Rivers Ranch Romance™ (Book 9): Sandy Keller is tired of the dating scene in Three Rivers. Though she owns the pancake house, she's looking for a fresh start, which means an escape from the town where she grew up. When her older brother's best friend, Tad Jorgensen, comes to town for the holidays, it is a balm to his weary soul. A helicopter tour guide who experienced a near-death experience, he's looking to start over too--but in Three Rivers. Can Sandy and Tad navigate their troubles to find the path God wants them to take--and discover true love--in only ten days?

Eleven Year Reunion: A Three Rivers Ranch Romance™ (Book 10): Pastry chef extraordinaire, Grace Lewis has moved to Three Rivers to help Heidi Ackerman open a bakery in Three Rivers. Grace relishes the idea of starting over in a town where no one knows about her failed cupcakery. She doesn't expect to run into her old high school boyfriend, Jonathan Carver. A carpenter working at Three Rivers Ranch, Jon's in town against his will. But with Grace now on the scene, Jon's thinking life in Three Rivers is suddenly looking up. But with her focus on baking and his disdain for small towns, can they make their eleven year reunion stick?

The Twelfth Town: A Three Rivers Ranch Romance™ (Book 11): Newscaster Taryn Tucker has had enough of life on-screen. She's bounced from town to town before arriving in Three Rivers, completely alone and completely anonymous--just the way she now likes it. She takes a job cleaning at Three Rivers Ranch, hoping for a chance to figure out who she is and where God wants her. When she meets happy-go-lucky cowhand Kenny Stockton, she doesn't expect sparks to fly. Kenny's always been "the best friend" for his female friends, but the pull between him and Taryn can't be denied. Will they have the courage and faith necessary to make their opposite worlds mesh?

Lucky Number Thirteen: A Three Rivers Ranch Romance™ (Book 12): Tanner Wolf, a rodeo champion ten times over, is excited to be riding in Three Rivers for the first time since he left his philandering ways and found religion. Seeing his old friends Ethan and Brynn is therapuetic--until a terrible accident lands him in the hospital. With his rodeo career over, Tanner thinks maybe he'll stay in town--and it's not just because his nurse, Summer Hamblin, is the prettiest woman he's ever met. But Summer's the queen of first dates, and as she looks for a way to make a relationship with the transient rodeo star work Summer's not sure she has the fortitude to go on a second date. Can they find love among the tragedy?

The Curse of February Fourteenth: A Three Rivers Ranch Romance™ (Book 13): Cal Hodgkins, cowboy veterinarian at Bowman's Breeds, isn't planning to meet anyone at the masked dance in small-town Three Rivers. He just wants to get his bachelor friends off his back and sit on the sidelines to drink his punch. But when he sees a woman dressed in gorgeous butterfly wings and cowgirl boots with blue stitching, he's smitten. Too bad she runs away from the dance before he can get her name, leaving only her boot behind...

Fifteen Minutes of Fame: A Three Rivers Ranch Romance™ (Book 14): Navy Richards is thirty-five years of tired— tired of dating the same men, working a demanding job, and getting her heart broken over and over again. Her aunt has always spoken highly of the matchmaker in Three Rivers, Texas, so she takes a six-month sabbatical from her high-stress job as a pediatric nurse, hops on a bus, and meets with the matchmaker. Then she meets Gavin Redd. He's handsome, he's hardworking, and he's a cowboy. But is he an Aquarius too? Navy's not making a move until she knows for sure...

Sixteen Steps to Fall in Love: A Three Rivers Ranch Romance™ (Book 15): A chance encounter at a dog park sheds new light on the tall, talented Boone that Nicole can't ignore. As they get to know each other better and start to dig into each other's past, Nicole is the one who wants to run. This time from her growing admiration and attachment to Boone. From her aging parents. From herself.

But Boone feels the attraction between them too, and he decides he's tired of running and ready to make Three Rivers his permanent home. **Can Boone and Nicole use their faith to overcome their differences and find a happily-ever-after together?**

The Sleigh on Seventeenth Street: A Three Rivers Ranch Romance™ (Book 16): A cowboy with skills as an electrician tries a relationship with a down-on-her luck plumber. Can Dylan and Camila make water and electricity play nicely together this Christmas season? Or will they get shocked as they try to make their relationship work?

The First Lady of Three Rivers Ranch: A Three Rivers Ranch Romance™ (Book 17): Heidi Duffin has been dreaming about opening her own bakery since she was thirteen years old. She scrimped and saved for years to afford baking and pastry school in San Francisco. And now she only has one year left before she's a certified pastry chef. Frank Ackerman's father has recently retired, and he's taken over the largest cattle ranch in the Texas Panhandle. A horseman through and through, he's also nearing thirty-one and looking for someone to bring love and joy to a homestead that's been dominated by men for a decade. But when he convinces Heidi to come clean the cowboy cabins, she changes all that. But the siren's call of a bakery is still loud in Heidi's ears, even if she's also seeing a future with Frank. Can she rely on her faith in ways she's never had to before or will their relationship end when summer does?

Second Generation in Three Rivers Romance™ Series

Step back into the heartwarming small Texas town of Three Rivers! This beloved town has captured the hearts of 2.5 million readers and caught the eye of Sony Pictures, and now a new generation of cowboys and cowgirls is ready to take center stage. Scan the QR code below with your phone to check out this new series!

1. The Cowboy Who Came Home - featuring Squire's son, Finn from SECOND CHANCE RANCH!

Seven Sons Ranch in Three Rivers Romance™ Series

Meet the cowboy billionaire brothers at Seven Sons Ranch! Scan the QR code below with your phone to check out this complete series.

1. Rhett's Make-Believe Marriage
2. Tripp's Trivial Tie
3. Liam's Invented I-Do
4. Jeremiah's Bogus Bride
5. Wyatt's Pretend Pledge
6. Skyler's Wanna-Be Wife
7. Micah's Mock Matrimony
8. Gideon's Precious Penny

Shiloh Ridge Ranch in Three Rivers Romance™ Series

Meet the cowboy billionaires in the southern hills outside of Three Rivers! Scan the QR code below with your phone to check out this complete series.

1. The Mechanics of Mistletoe
2. The Horsepower of the Holiday
3. The Construction of Cheer
4. The Secret of Santa
5. The Gift of Gingerbread
6. The Harmony of Holly
7. The Chemistry of Christmas
8. The Delivery of Decor
9. The Blessing of Babies
10. The Networking of the Nativity
11. The Wrangling of the Wreath
12. The Hope of Her Heart

About Liz

Liz Isaacson writes inspirational romance, usually set in Texas, or Wyoming, or anywhere else horses and cowboys exist. She lives in Utah, where she writes full-time, takes her two dogs to the park everyday, and eats a lot of veggies while writing. Find all of her books on her website at feelgoodfictionbooks.com.